THE WATERSHED PROJECT

DAVID NORMAN

Black Rose Writing | Texas

ISBN: 978-1-68433-722-4
PUBLISHED BY BLACK ROSE WRITING
www.blackrosewriting.com

Printed in the United States of America
Suggested Retail Price (SRP) $18.95

The Watershed Project is printed in Palatino Linotype

For my parents,
Alice and James Norman,
and in memory of Blanca Sermeno

THE WATERSHED
PROJECT

"When two people quit leaning on Christ to unite them with His Love, they're like two different parts talking at the same time."

—**Zacharias P. Hembrey**

"*Invention* can refer to a type of musical composition, a falsehood, a discovery, or any product of the imagination."

—*Merriam-Webster's Dictionary*

PREFACE TO THE NEW EDITION

Despite my daughter's claims, I left this new edition intact. Small edits in the radio-broadcast portion of our narrative were made to facilitate a smoother reading experience. The task of editing one's speech from an earlier time, preserving one's opinions that may seem arrogant or ludicrous in the context of What We Know Today, presented a special challenge.

You will hear opinions I no longer hold. You will witness erroneous deeds I no longer commit. I believe in the power of the Almighty to change our lives. The Lord has changed mine. As for Elizabeth's letters to her friend, this improved new edition leaves her words untouched. Let me be clear: I did not meddle with what my daughter said.

Respecting the wishes of the widow Mrs. Valenkemp, I have removed all letters written by her daughter Nelle to Elizabeth, including the one in which Nelle refers to my daughter as a "devil child." Special thanks to my Praise Team for their help translating the letters Elizabeth wrote to Nelle in a dialect of Biblical Hebrew for the express purpose of mocking the father who taught her the Holy language of Ancient Israel and of hiding certain facts.

In this new edition, I maintain Elizabeth's punctuation of dialogue, which uses dashes for character speech and quotation marks for sarcasm and other phrases not attributable to characters in the story (i.e., Holy Scripture). If anybody feels I wasn't faithful to the first edition, I apologize. Luckily, nobody has read the first edition. I own every copy. Individuals who recorded the radio-broadcast portion with their tape decks or other such home-stereo systems—beware. Unauthorized sharing, copying, or distributing of this material is a violation of federal law. In other words, if you try anything funny, I will sue you for piracy. To the good Christian folks who missed the live version, don't worry. This new edition covers it all.

By the grace of God, we now have access to the Truth. After careful, *careful* editing, we can hear the words of Elizabeth Hembrey with our own eyes, see the words of Pastor Zacharias Patrick Hembrey with our own ears, and we can form our own opinions. God bless our country and its common language, English, and may He no longer fear our power to Unify.

When we work together, nothing is impossible. Amen.

NOTE ON THE PREFACE TO THE NEW EDITION

If my dad gives you his address for general inquiries, don't bother. It's not a fake address, but his wife Lourna, my mom, who plays the role of secretary in our little domestic drama, has been instructed not to write to anyone unless they show up at church and fill out one of those information cards that require a "few bits" of information such as your first and last name, your phone number, your address, social security number, birth certificate, and anything else you'd like to share under the space marked "other." Don't do it. I'm warning you.

If you *are* crazy enough to fill out one of my dad's info cards, partially or fully, Pastor Zacharias will unleash his Prayer Partners on you with a mighty vengeance. They will harass you with phone calls. They will stick junk flyers in your mailbox. They will knock on your door. If you don't answer your door, they will return. Heaven help us.

The info cards say, "Welcome Home." They *should* say, "Welcome to Hell."

By "small edits" in the radio broadcast, my dad means the times he used profanity on air or else blatantly contradicted himself. Don't worry, I get the last word here. I'm restoring all of his embarrassing and hypocritical behavior into the "new" edition.

Honestly, he did buy every copy of the first edition so nobody could read them. He threatened to sue his Christian publishers if they tried to sell or distribute any additional books. All of the first editions are in our garage, in boxes sealed with duct tape. He never wants these books to see the light of day, and yet he never got rid of them. Interesting.

Skeletons in the garage.

Also, when he thanks his Praise Team for "translating" the Biblical Hebrew into English, are you kidding me? I wrote those letters in

Biblical Hebrew for *him*, to let him know I knew he was snooping, reading what he shouldn't have been reading (i.e., my letters to Nelle).

Anyway, it wasn't real Hebrew. I'm not that smart. It was a system of *alef-bet* letters that replaced the English, a code anybody with a sixth-grade education could crack. It's not what he changed, it's what he *misheard* that infuriates me. "Careful editing"? Give me a break.

Take the title, for example. That was *my* title. But he took out the punctuation marks. It should say *Watershed, Project!* Like, Go ahead, *project* your version of events onto mine.

I disagree with him, but I'm willing to listen to what he has to say.

Small edits? I might be fourteen, but I'm smart enough to recognize Censorship. Don't worry. Like I said before, we're working through our issues. I'll correct his speech and remove a sly redaction when I spot one. No edition can "cover everything," but at least we can hear different opinions. At least we don't have to silence voices that don't conform to some Unified Body of Christianity, or whatever. As a pastor my dad should know, God confused the people of Babel with their language and scattered them abroad for good reason.

Nobody should have *that* much power.

HOW TO GET IN TOUCH WITH THE LORD

You go down Main Street until you don't see the Annie's Antiques or the DQ. Now, you should've passed Veterans Memorial Park already, and you should definitely no longer see the Daylight Donuts. That's more in the center of town. Fact is, you won't see much of anything except the scrub oak and a goat farm and a real bad sinkhole up near the top of the hill, but don't worry about it. If you're at the top of the hill, you've gone too far.

The windmill will appear on your left. Past that windmill, there's an open road that's rutted all to hell and looks like nobody's used it in decades except a tractor or a combine. You take that road, turn left. It doesn't look like any road a map would want to display in proper letters. Halfway down you'll see smoke from a busted chimenea. New neighbors finally wised up and burn their own dead wood instead of buying from the store. Waste of money.

This Sunday Franklin Road's gonna be covered in raccoon shit, I'm afraid, near where it hooks up with Main. Somebody doesn't know the first thing about proper pest control. Normally, I'd say Fred Valenkemp left his Fritos on the porch rail, crumbs for the night critters. —Eating Fritos corn chips is what he's doing, not writing Beethoven's Tenth Symphony. But Fred's no longer with us. Our keyboardist, I loved him to death, so I always cut him some slack. An insomniac, Fred composed at night, so he might have seen the raccoons, who all outlived him. Yes, that rutted-racoon shit road where Main Street runs out of its mind? That's Franklin.

I'd give you a street address, but it doesn't matter. You won't need it.

The barn at the bottom of the cul-de-sac? That's Watershed. Y'all feel free to park in Rachel's grass. It's her grass now, not Fred's. Don't worry about messing up the jasmine or the mums. I got special permission for y'all to park in Rachel's grass. Hallelujah.

Pull your trucks all the way forward against the cedar logs so we can fit everybody in. It's gonna be a big crowd. You know Rachel never had seen a windmill before she moved here? Well, that's another story. The Bible says God saw you in your mother's womb.

We at the Watershed Project believe God's vision of you, inside your mother's womb, a slimy tadpole at eight weeks, includes a special plan. A script for your entire life only He knows and all you have to do is open your heart to Jesus and He will show you the Way.

In this part of the sermon, if I weren't on the radio, I'd crouch like I'm ready to catch a baseball, I'd pump both my fists, and with my eyes shut tight like I'm taking a holy crap, I'd lean my head back and scream at the ceiling. JESUS WILL SHOW YOU THE WAY!

Only we don't have a ceiling, it's just wood rafters.

Doesn't matter, y'all. I'm so confident He will show you the way, I can't say it loud enough: Hey, buddy, rub the dust off your soul. You're worth something. You are God's ambassador. You're the head and not the tail. And this here's my tale. My name is Pastor Zacharias Patrick Hembrey, and if you come down to the Watershed Project, I'll tell you how I survived the Alejandro Brothers. Big Alejandro and Little Alejandro. That's right. I'll tell you how we were like the myth of the Phoenix, this church. How this blue barn with a beautiful new cross on the top of its steeple burst into flames and rose again from its ashes.

Born Again.

Whatever you've been facing this week, you'll find the answer by celebrating with us in the House of the Lord. We used to call ourselves Watershed Church, but now we're the Watershed Project. We're a work-in-progress. We believe in the love and compassion of Jesus Christ. It might not have seemed like love and compassion when my daughter's dog ran out the back of the church with its tail on fire. You ask Fred for caviar, he'll give you Fritos corn chips. Don't let the fancy suit and expensive watch fool you. Listen to me, jumping ahead of myself and talking about Fred Valenkemp in the present tense, like he's still alive.

WHERE I FOUND SHADOW, THE MUTT

Dear Nelle, My dad doesn't actually know if Shadow, our black-furred mutt, made it out alive. While I can picture Shadow running out of the church with her tail on fire, it's also possible my dad invented the image for his listeners and to make me feel better by giving me Hope. The fact of the matter is no one saw Shadow escape. All the firetrucks were parked out front, shoved together inside the cul-de-sac. Not one of the firefighters said, Hey, check out that dog with its tail on fire. Shadow often slept in the church, so she was probably inside that night, sleeping under the lectern, and if Shadow fled out the front door she'd have shot past the firemen who were busy trying to attach their hoses to the broken fire hydrant. We got a new one, by the way. A new hydrant. Red with a little orange flag on top like the ones up north where it snows.

I guess it's illegal to have no source of water for putting out fires.

Not that you'd care, Nelle. After what I did to your dad, you'll probably never return to Watershed, unless your mom drags you, which frankly I don't see happening. Our church is a scorched battlefield of broken families. Married men attend service without their wives, and wives attend without their husbands. I know I sound like a hypocrite, being a regular church member and all, but technically I'm still a child. The pastor's daughter doesn't get to choose whether she wants to attend or not. I knew this guy Sanford, a regular member, whose wife allowed him to go as long as he didn't bring the Bible talk home with him. That sounds like a healthy compromise. You can listen and pray, but don't bring all the crazy stuff home.

My family adopted Shadow from a shelter in Pleasanton when she was eight weeks old. She's part blood hound, part Lab. When I get out of Warm Springs, I'm going to put up some flyers and search the neighborhood. Maybe somebody kidnapped her. We brought her with us when we moved from San Antonio. Shadow preferred the church over our tiny house. She'd drink water out of the flower pots. She'd drink from the sidewalk puddles. She'd lick the rain gutters. She'd slurp from any place except her bowl. She knew how to find water. Maybe that's part of her hunting instincts, I don't know. She must have smelled the smoke, and if she ran out the back, she probably *was* on fire, but I like to think she'd know where to find enough water to extinguish herself. Animals hide when they're injured. Maybe she's hiding.

One time a neighbor fired his shotgun at a raccoon in his back yard, and his shot cleared the fence, and one of the little shotgun pellets hit Shadow in the hind leg. This neighbor had terrible aim, obviously. The raccoon escaped, but Shadow got hit. She hid behind the ficus for hours. I had to lure her out with a rib bone. She's been through a lot. I guess we all have.

Sorry, I'll stop talking about Shadow. Makes me sad thinking of her. I really hope she turns up in the end, but like my shrink says, favorable outcomes are beyond my control.

THE LOCK-IN

Good morning, Watershed. Normally in this part of the service I'd have my daughter Elizabeth do the announcements. She'd say good morning, Watershed! And she'd put her hand to her ear and smile and wait for everybody to say, Good morning! And I should admit right now, before I continue, some of you out there know this anyway—Elizabeth is back in the hospital.

I don't like to think of her at Warm Springs, pacing up and down the hall in her pale-blue robe and green socks. After we had her admitted, *Elizabeth* admitted something to her best friend, Nelle, a piece of news I still find astonishing and sad. Elizabeth said if she'd participated in the Lock-in, she'd have stepped directly into the flames in order to immolate herself on the altar of Our Lord Jesus. "Immolate," that was the word she'd used. It's a big word, and she's a smart girl, and I don't doubt she understands what it means. She probably overheard someone say it at Warm Springs while she padded down the hall in her socks and robe.

I don't like to think about all the people in there, fallen people, who're low in the eyes of Our Lord, who're no doubt swapping tales of previous suicide attempts. Immolating, hanging, shooting, jumping. Attempts by pills, by knife, by gun. Plastic bag around the head, in the garage with the car door closed, motor running. Off a bridge or an apartment building, not high enough. Blunt razor blade, or what have you. The sinful acts of fallen individuals. And among them, my precious daughter. Who's doing wonderful, by the way. Wonderful. No further announcements at this time on the matter of her mental and spiritual health. But we *will* be participating in the 9th Annual Heal the Soul Fun Walk, 5K Run and 10K Run. Mark your calendars. March 3rd at 8AM. The Prayer & Worship Committee will NOT be able to cover your registration fee unless you register before February 10th! Also, please provide your name, your chosen event, and T-shirt size to my wife Lourna in the church office. I don't know what the shirts will look like. She'll have the design ready once we get closer to race time.

I should also mention Lourna's going to take over the announcements until Elizabeth gets out of the hospital. Lourna can do the announcements for as long as we need her. No problem. Why not let Rachel Valenkemp tackle announcements? Well, Rachel's handled enough. Nobody knows what Rachel had to go through with her husband Fred, who has passed on from this world. Yes, I told you already, and I'll say it again. Fred is dead. Nobody knows the pain Rachel suffered at the hands of her dead husband. Nobody knows her mind, either, like I did, the time she revealed it to me at Freedom Keys Music School under the auspices of Our Lord Jesus. (More on this later.) Nobody could have known what dark motives lay beneath the surface of the mind of the man I loved like a brother, Fred Valenkemp. Elizabeth has her theory, but I would caution you against trusting what she says this early in the game. Her mind is not well.

The doctors are helping her remember this thing correctly.

We'll be doing the clothing drive again this fall. I wasn't happy with last year's effort, but it's a new year. So please bring your gently worn items, especially your hats with no holes and your gloves with all ten fingers, to the green bins outside Freedom Keys. You can't miss those green bins. I kid you not, Lourna put them in the doorway. Parents, your children will have to scoot their butts around the bins if they want to get inside. The kids will have the pleasure of staring into those bins in an attempt to fathom the Human Tragedy of Poverty in this Country before they can gather in a circle on the rug, crisscross apple sauce, and sing "This is The Day."

The Lock-in will take place on November 8th again, that's a Saturday. I don't know why we do this during flu season, folks. And I don't know why we still call it a Lock-in. Nobody ever locks the doors.

Some kids will not show up. They're sick. Some kids will show up. Their parents didn't realize their kids were sick. Sick, or not sick. Okay? Parents, please make sure your children are fever free for at least twenty-four hours before bringing them to the Watershed Project on the night of November 8th.

If this were an actual sermon, I'd stress this point in the name of Christ Jesus: I welcome all children to my church. Let the little children come unto Watershed. You'll hear how the music school brought in more cash than our offerings and tithes combined. It surprised me how much parents would pay for the promise of turning their kids into little Mozarts. The kids who participated in the Lock-in the night of the explosion all got out safely. No dead children in this broadcast, folks, but I did expect twelve kids that year. Only eight showed, and I had to send two home with their bed rolls and their backpacks because Lourna had a thermometer.

Fever free.

Before Watershed started burning, board games were allowed for the Lock-in as long as they were age-appropriate. We're not doing board games this year. We're going to have Bible study and Bible songs. Sorry, I don't have to remind you about how our Leader of Youth Ministries told me to go home that night.

—You sure? I said. I can read them Genesis in the original Hebrew.

—No, Pastor. Enjoy your night. We got it covered.

So I went home. Later that night, I visited some of the more severe cases in the burn ward. Not from our church. These were from the Travelodge that caught fire weeks earlier, I think. Main thing is nobody burns in Watershed. In Watershed, we're all saved in the name of Christ Jesus. But there was this one patient. A nervous man. A non-believer. Middle-aged, or probably younger. All his hair burned up in the fire. This anxious little man asked me what it would be like to die. Without hesitation I said to him it's like going home.

—Do we have any new visitors with us this morning?

Normally in this part of the service, we'll get one or two hands, or three hands if we're lucky. We'll send the ushers over with the info cards for them to fill out. New members are essential to the survival of the Watershed Project. —What do we tell our new visitors?

And the crowd replies, Welcome Home!

—That's right. You're home. You've been wandering. Now you're home.

It's called "asking the question." Sometimes a front-row regular will raise his or her hand to remind me to do the welcome-home speech. They're so considerate. They'll whisper, Pastor, you forgot to ask the question. And I'll say, Oh, yes, what do we tell our new visitors?

One of our landlord's cows got loose. If you think the smell of manure is bad, you should have smelled the church that night. The smell dug into my nostrils while the smoke stung my eyes, and the fire roared in my ears. I was a moth running at the flames.

Parked my Chevy as close to the cul-de-sac as I could get, leapt out in my pajamas, and high-knee'd it over the fire hoses, which swelled like pythons. Yes, sometimes a fire hose is only a fire hose, but if y'all would please keep the backstage door closed, use the lobby doors if you have to go to your car, if you need to smoke a cigarette, or leave for any reason during the sermon? That would help with the smell. There are church fires, and there are church fires. This one rolled diabolically. The steeple smoldered and collapsed. At some point in the night, after running in my pajamas, I stumbled and fell in the yard. The fire roared above me and the sirens wailed at my back, and I couldn't hear them say everyone got out, I couldn't have heard the words if somebody had screamed them in my ears. No, sir. I couldn't hear a thing.

Most of you remember my daughter Elizabeth. She didn't participate in the Lock-in because we'd admitted her to Warm Springs the day before. Jesus, not her madness, spared her from the flames. She's back at Warm Springs, where she writes letters to her best friend, Nelle. Letters which I intercept. Oh, don't worry, you'll hear from Elizabeth. She will try to convince you she killed Fred Valenkemp herself. The doctors are helping her remember this thing correctly. But it's important we give her the space to tell her story, which will differ slightly from the *his*-story of these tragic events.

Nothing inside to burn like that. We had clothes from the clothing drive. We had our stage equipment: amplifiers, quarter-inch cables, the drum set, the stage lights. We had hay from the previous year's nativity scene, but still. Nothing to burn the way Watershed did.

THE ADULT IN THE ROOM

Dear Nelle, Need I remind you I am not a religious person? I do not have my father's zeal for the whole redemption story. The ballads we sang during the service? Those were all love songs to Jesus. Which is kind of weird when you think about it. Taking a rock ballad by some hair band, turning down the electric guitars, turning up the synthesizers, and swapping out the boyfriend for Jesus? It's one thing to dress up as Jesus for some ridiculous fall festival, another thing to make Jesus your romantic partner for life. To sexualize Jesus. Woah, hold up.

"I need you." And, "Your spirit moves in me." And, "You conquer me." The female vocalists in our Praise Team could really croon. They'd sing these songs with such passion. They'd clench their fists, raise their arms to the sky, pound their thighs. They'd rock back and forth on their feet, sway side to side. They all looked so constipated. What exactly did they want Jesus to do to them? How exactly did they want Jesus to move or conquer them?

"You touch me, and I am touched." And, "Your way works through me."

I don't have to tell you, the implication of those lyrics is pretty gross. What we did to your dad's studio was pretty gross, too, but he deserved it. I'm glad you're still my friend even though I killed him. I say this without fear of punishment because I no longer believe in hell. I killed your dad. I killed Fred Valenkemp. Wow. How liberating! My confession should go into a song. I could make up some bad-ass lyrics. By writing about what happened between me and your dad, the private stuff, I can fill in the gaps and remind you how fathers can be such a drag.

I'm glad you're still my friend. I said that already, didn't I?

Remember when we took the cinderblocks off the garbage can lids to see what animals could get into the garbage outside your dad's studio? You should do that again. Sorry, but I don't believe mountain lions roam the hill country. My dad got spiritually diverted in South Padre Island when I was four. I don't remember. Mom could tell you about South Padre, but she may not talk to you on account of your being Rachel Valenkemp's daughter. You might think I'm crazy, but I have to side with Mom here. Rachel got too close to my dad, plain and simple, almost destroyed our family. If I were Dad, I wouldn't allow Rachel back at church. Dad's problem is he's too caught up in the ceremonial aspects of Watershed. All his normally-in-this-part-of-the-service digressions. He should've listened to his own family instead of Rachel. Definitely never listened to me, although he made a good effort of pretending.

I wouldn't trust any church that would have my dad for a leader, but Watershed was and is our livelihood. Watershed brought home the bacon. I understand Rachel played a Role.

THE PRAYER BEFORE THE OFFERING

So the kids were spending the night. It was the Lock-in. Y'all already know we didn't really lock the doors. We called it a Lock-in because the event used to take place near the end of October, on the same night as a certain pagan holiday I won't mention.

"Lock-in" sounded spookier than "sleepover." Kids dressed up in costumes of their favorite Bible character, and they played games and ate popcorn and candy. We had a lot of Jesuses. Jesuses in Birkenstocks with sheets like togas wrapped around their skinny torsos. We had shepherd's crooks made out of empty toilet paper rolls. Thorny crowns made out of paper mâché. We had cherry pie filling for the blood He shed for your sins smeared all over those little Jesuses. We don't let the kids dress up anymore. Costumes encourage immoral behavior. Now we call the October gathering a "fall festival," and Lourna gets the kids to cut maple leaves out of orange construction paper and decorate the leaves with glitter. The sleepover got moved up to November 8th, the gut middle of flu season. And we're still calling it a Lock-in.

Normally in this part of the service, I'd loosen up the crowd with some physical comedy. I'd stumble across the stage, pretend to fall off the edge. I'd do a somersault, leap into the air and spread my arms, then pound my chest like a gorilla.

We're heading into the Prayer Before the Offering, a time when we call on the generosity of our guests to pull out their wallets and purses and show their Love for Jesus. A lighter mood encourages giving. So do threats of eternal damnation, but I prefer the lighter, comedic route. For all I know, I'm asking some homeless veteran, and we've had many in our flock, to fork over his last greasy Abe Lincoln to keep the

Watershed Project afloat. Never mind what the veteran's gonna eat. We'll break more bread. We'll find a way to feed them all.

Remember the rich man in the Bible who thought he could pull down his barn and build a bigger one to store all his grain and all his goods? The Lord said to him, "You fool! This very night your life is being demanded of you." Do not store up your goods, folks. We're not gonna build a bigger barn here. We're settling with the one we have. It's a beautiful barn. The Lord will take care of us. You just have to give. Give and receive the mercy of Almighty Jesus.

Did I mention the Alejandro Brothers? Big Alejandro and Little Alejandro. They wanted to store their grain in my barn. Only theirs wasn't grain and mine wasn't just a barn. They demanded to pack kilos of their grain into so many hidden places inside my church you wouldn't believe. Nearly destroyed us, trying to keep all their grain hidden before the eyes of the Lord. Yes, I let them do it. I was the fool whose life they demanded. And the lives of my family.

Was I the Rich Man off relaxing on South Padre Island? (Here's where I lie down on the stage, relax, and pretend to suntan my arms. I pretend to sip a fancy tropical beverage with a colorful straw, pineapple slice, and paper umbrella.)

Usually we get a few chuckles, then I jump up and shout, What a fool!

Now I leave my character of Rich Man. I grab my hair and moan. I'm Penitent Man. (Y'all can't see since we're on the air, but I have nice thick hair. No pastor has thicker hair than Zacharias Patrick Hembrey.) And so I grab my hair and make my hair stand up on my head like a clutch of Communist wheat. If my congregants don't laugh, my Praise Team will laugh for them. I pay my Praise Team to laugh on command. It's in their job description.

—The Bible says, "So it is with those who store up treasures for themselves but are not rich toward God." —Yes, sir. We ask you to hold out your offerings and pray. Pray for my daughter Elizabeth, that she makes it out of Warm Springs. We don't use the word "asylum" anymore, but step inside Warm Springs for an hour or two, and the word "asylum" will clap in your head like a bell. The night of the explosion, Elizabeth was supposed to be in church. To save the children, I became a moth running at the flames.

I ran through fire to save half a dozen lambs.

Elizabeth was my mother-in-law's first name. Lourna's mother died of pancreatic cancer the year before Jesus blessed us with our baby girl. At the time, we didn't know Elizabeth in the Bible was Zacharias's wife, and I didn't call myself Zacharias, I was plain Zach. We weren't true Christians yet. Please don't go making associations.

Lourna said she wanted her baby to know her grandma. The name "Elizabeth" would remind us to talk to the baby about Grandma Liz. Thirteen years went by before the night Watershed Church exploded, and I could count the number of times we talked about Grandma Liz on one hand. Why are we afraid to speak of the dead in this country? Lourna and I love our daughter. Taking her out of San Antonio might have been a mistake.

We are fearfully and wonderfully made. The Lord writes all our days for us in His Book before they exist. When we first moved here, Salterra didn't welcome us. Nobody could read what kind of days lay ahead. I wondered what Elizabeth thought of her new home.

NOT QUITE THE BEST DONUTS IN TOWN

Nelle, I don't agree with my dad about our church having the best donuts. Dad doesn't go to Daylight Donuts because it's too long a drive. So his donuts come from the H-E-B on the interstate. They're store-bought glazed. Yet he drove to Daylight to meet Rachel for coffee, and the sheriff stopped him in the parking lot? Sheriff Lufkin stopped him to say there was a noise complaint and someone left the lights on at Freedom Keys?

I find that weird, Nelle. My dad driving to meet Rachel, I mean.

Sorry I'm calling your mom "Rachel" and not "Mrs. Valenkemp" like I did when I came to your house and we drank peach schnapps on the roof of your father's studio. I never called her "Rachel" in person, you know. I didn't call your dad anything except "Fred," "Mr. Valenkemp," or maybe "Satan" if he caught me in one of my moods.

Names are important in the Bible, but I'm also trying to avoid pronoun confusion. If I'd been born a boy, my parents would have named me John. Not after Headless John. The other one, the Apostle. Remember the lake? Whoops, I'm getting ahead of myself.

You told me about Houston, so I'll tell you about Salterra, the hell we found ourselves in. Salt of the Earth. Yeah, right. These people didn't flock to Watershed. Salterra already had three churches, something Pastor Zacharias failed to realize when we left San Antonio to become tenants in a tiny roach-infested house with two bedrooms, one bathroom, and no central air.

What'd my dad do wrong? He poached all his congregants from New Foundations, the mega-church we'd been attending in San Antonio since I was four. Church leaders at New Foundations were furious, and I wouldn't be surprised if it turns out they're the ones who tipped off Lester Hargreve and the Alejandro Brothers, but I'll save that story for another letter.

If I don't go to college, I'll become a bricklayer. If I go, I'll major in psychology.

OVERBEARING ABOUT THE TREATS

Not that I'm a control freak, but I kind of need to oversee every aspect of the service before the whole thing falls apart. The store-bought glazed donuts my daughter complains about are there for a reason. The sugar icing has already formed a hard shell around the fried dough which doesn't leave a hot gooey mess all over your fingers and clothes. During the Peace Offering, our congregants make it a point (I make it their point, actually) to shake the hands of every soul in their row. Can you imagine the mess? How many napkins we'd go through?

—Peace be with you, brother. Also, that glob of cinnamon icing I left on your bright Tommy Hilfiger. Sorry, sister, I stained the silk collar of your Sunday dress, etc.

Not to act like an overlord, but the Lipton iced tea must not be flavored.

Whoever snuck in raspberry that one morning needs to be reminded of the rules. Do not sneak in raspberry or black currant tea, folks. People don't like surprises. Keep it simple with the tea: sweetened and unsweetened. Two metal bins with black spigots, and put some green tape on the container like I taught you, one layer of green tape, so they know it's the sweet stuff.

Same with the coffee: Set up the two big silver coffee urns on the table, regular and decaf. Don't get cute with blueberry, vanilla, or caramel-spice coffee. Disgusting flavors. And put napkins under the spigots so we don't leak all over the brochures. Will you do this for me, please? Keep it simple. Green tape, iced tea, coffee, store-bought glazed. Hallelujah.

If y'all want to bring your own thermoses that's fine, but we can't serve cups larger than the eight-ounce Polystyrenes I've written on the church grocery list. Eight ounces, okay? This isn't a coffee shop. We're not here to stand in the lobby all morning ingesting caffeine. Eight ounces. You swallow your eight ounces, or pour the dregs into the water fountain if you've had enough, scarf down a store-bought glazed (limit your enjoyment to one donut if you're one of the early arrivals, as we want to make sure everybody gets at least one donut), and then go find a seat in the sanctuary. This is Watershed. We're family. We're also a business. I know y'all don't want to hear this part, but it's true. We're on a budget. No, we can't afford the fancy insulated cups with the American flags on them. Yes, they make you feel patriotic, yes, they don't scald your hands, but those cups are too expensive for Watershed, and with twelve ounces—or God forbid, sixteen ounces—of a caffeinated beverage sloshing around in your bladder, you're gonna have folks running off to the commode every five seconds and that presents a problem. With everybody getting up all the time, I wouldn't have my perfect silence to deliver God's message.

Sneezing and coughing's fine to a certain extent. But do y'all really need to cough so many times? Do you need to blow your nose with such obnoxious honking into your bandana? Yes, I understand about flu season. I just need my audience to do two things: I need y'all to listen, and I need y'all to concentrate. Transform yourselves into quiet receptacles ready for the Holy Spirit. The Holy Spirit shall enter if you shut your mouths for a moment and open your hearts wide enough. Yes, Jesus will speak through me to deliver His Message regardless, even if you foolishly decide not to take your wailing infants to the crying room, but this whole thing works better if y'all obey the rules. This whole thing works better if y'all pay *attention*.

NOBODY WAS PAYING ATTENTION

I wasn't paying attention when my parents drove me to the hospital, but I do remember the night I spent under observation in the ER. Blood on my T-shirt, and I couldn't stop shaking. For some reason, they wouldn't transfer me to Warm Springs right away. They needed to contact our insurance company to make sure I was still covered. Had I exceeded the number of stays? My card punched too many times? It's funny how I spent the night in a hospital chair with a sheet that wouldn't cover me. I mean, it couldn't keep me warm because it was too small. When I pulled it up around my shoulders, my feet stuck out. When I tucked it around my feet, my shoulders and neck lay exposed. I felt like a grasshopper on a dissection tray.

The central air blew down over me in the waiting room they'd locked me in, a room no bigger than my bedroom at home. The man behind the observation window apologized. He had no control.

—Must be up to God, I said. (He didn't laugh.) The air temperature dropped every hour. The whole night, he would read or pretend to read a crime novel and drink coffee from a paper cup, anything to make it seem like he wasn't there to watch me.

Every now and then, he'd pick up the phone and call the number on the back of my father's insurance card. Congratulations, Pastor Zacharias, for purchasing *the* cheapest insurance policy in the world. But why buy decent insurance when you've turned your life over to Christ? When you've put Jesus in the driver's seat? The paper insurance card had one of those one eight-hundred numbers with no hint of an actual human on the other end of the line, only a long string of recorded messages. If you'd like to speak to God, please press "0" followed by the "#" key.

—Sorry about the room, the man said. It's the best we could do.

—It's all right. As long as it's temporary.

—Only for tonight. So, we good? You're not going to do anything stupid?

—No, I've already gotten stupid out of my system.

Honestly, Nelle, that RN was less concerned about my mental state than about making sure his shift went smoothly. He wanted no trouble on his watch. Meanwhile, to pass the time, I imagined myself pulling a Sarah Connor like in *Terminator 2: Judgement Day* when she busts out of the asylum with a syringe full of blue Drano or whatever held against her psychiatrist's neck. I didn't have a psychiatrist. Not yet. I had a guy watching me or not watching behind a little glass window. I realized I'd rather pay my dues at Warm Springs than in prison for killing your dad, Fred Valenkemp. I wanted Time in the Ward to bring me some closure, or maybe not.

What I know now is my dad never wanted to help me get well for my own sake but for the sake of the church. He couldn't have a crazy daughter. He needed a model Christian girl to make the daily announcements, set up the donuts and coffee, hand out flyers, paint the stage Mars black. He didn't care about *me*. All he cared about was his stupid church.

Gusts of cold air hummed through the metal vents and blanketed my shoulders. The guy behind the window called my insurance company again and hung up. One time he came in and gave me a cup of hot cocoa. It tasted like mud but I thanked him. The chair I spent the night in was a fold-out that didn't fold out. A cushion made of concrete. It's a feat of engineering, Nelle. You have to go to a special school to learn how to make these uncomfortable chairs.

If I don't major in psychology, I'll become an engineer. I'll major in industrial design. I'll make a better chair for the cell they put you in before you're admitted to the psych ward.

I AM NO KING DAVID

After I spent the night duct-taped to a chair in a warehouse with Lester Hargreve pointing a gun at my face, telling me what the Alejandro Brothers might or might not do regarding the storage of their product in my church, I found myself tossed out of a moving car onto a soft patch of St. Augustine grass. A dog trotted over and licked my face. Shadow. I was home.

Lester and his men sped away in their car, and Lourna came out of the house, took off my blindfold and helped me off the ground. —Oh my God. Are you all right?

—I'm fine. I stood up, blinking, and tore the duct tape off my wrists. Terror in her face, which mirrored my own, registered in her eyebrows, pinched together, the two vertical lines forking away beneath her forehead, and in the way the half-moons of her irises sunk down, the whites of her eyes exposed above the irises, which I read as the visual equivalent of my wife Lourna screaming in terror. Also, I noticed a weapon tucked into her yoga pants.

—Is that a gun? I asked her. —Since when do you own a gun?

Lourna showed me her pistol, a baby pistol with a gold barrel and decorative ivory plates on the handle. It looked like something you'd keep with your pills or makeup kit. I guess that's the point: you pretend it's something cute and harmless. You keep its purpose hidden from yourself until you take it out to shoot at paper targets or kill someone.

—Sheriff Lufkin recommended I get one, Lourna said. For self-defense.

—Please, don't talk to the sheriff anymore. Stay away from the law.

—Zach, what happened? We need to go to the police.

I held her arms. —We can't tell anyone. Especially not Sheriff Lufkin.

Lourna looked like she was about to cry. —Okay, I won't.

—I need you to promise me.

—I promise.

—We'll keep this between us and God.

Lourna's cheeks turned blotchy, tears running down her face. I stared at the grass while Shadow whimpered against my leg.

—Anyway, it's safer if you don't know.

—Can you let me go? You're hurting me.

—I'm sorry. I released her.

—I'll keep this between us and God, she said.

—Okay, let's get inside. I need a shower.

My shower drained all the hot water in the tank, turned my skin pink, and after I got dressed I went to Watershed. Compared to the dreariness of the warehouse, the music room's primary colors—the red walls, the blue carpet, the yellow and green posters of the World's Musical Instruments—were loud and dizzying. I put my hand out and grabbed hold of the upright piano. The lid was cold. Its polish reflected the ceiling light.

Y'all remember the Baldwin Hamilton piano? Nice finish, elegant sound? Lourna and I found this piano outside the girls' dormitory at UTSA back when we were hunting for used furniture to make Watershed feel like Home.

—All the keys intact? I said to my wife. —No broken strings?

You gotta be kidding me.

Of course, we wouldn't need a piano anymore, not with my brother Fred and his electronic synthesizers. Even if we never used the Baldwin, I'd always thought you can't have a church, certainly not a music school, without a piano somewhere. But who knew you could remove the soundboard from a Baldwin Hamilton and use the extra space to store cocaine?

You see, I'd already put Jesus in the cockpit. He controlled my destiny. He molded my whole life before I was born. He knew my path. Whatever these drug lords wanted to do with me or my church, Jesus remained in control. So went my thoughts when I stepped into

Freedom Keys that morning, touched the lid of the Baldwin, and saw Fred's Fender Rhodes in the corner beside the conga drums, still in its suitcase, undisturbed. I dropped to the floor and prayed.

Call me some scripture. Somebody, please. Normally in this part of the service a pre-selected Prayer Partner will shout "Psalm 23!" or "First John 3:18!" And I'll recite the verse aloud from memory. What my congregants don't realize is we've already decided on that day's scripture. At Watershed, we leave nothing to chance.

That morning, I fell on my knees and said, "Little children," seeing as I'd found myself unable to exit the music room, "let us love, not in word or speech, but in truth and action."

In truth, I don't remember what verse I recited. I was too nervous. I was shaking all over. I'd showered after Lourna pulled me off the front lawn, but now the sweat broke across my forehead and my legs turned into the legs of a newborn gazelle.

From whence had this pressure descended over me? Please Lord, remove all demonic forces from the purity of Freedom Keys and keep our children safe. It's all about you, Lord, and none about me. They can take me anywhere, but don't let them harm the children.

—Teach me to love mine enemies.

—What enemies? Pastor, you all right?

A hand dropped upon my shoulder, and under the weight of this mysterious hand my body tingled with an usual wildness. It shook me out of my terror. It was the first time anyone, in my short life of forty-two years, had interrupted me mid-prayer. I turned to learn the owner of this hand, Rachel Valenkemp, who stared down at me with frightened eyes.

—Sorry, Pastor. She took her hand away and brought it to her mouth. —I didn't know what you were doing, whether you were praying or just talking to yourself. Let me help you up.

—Thank you.

Folks, I tried to rise on my own, honest, but my baby-deer legs wouldn't allow it. I was still shaking. I needed help. At first I thought the fright in her face had come from seeing me on the floor, but the way it lingered, the way the creases around her mouth and at the corners of her eyes thinned into almost nothing, like I've often read on the faces of the troubled before, led me to believe she had something on her mind long before my appearance that morning. She had faint Cleopatra marks at the corners of her eyes. Mascara? I knew she'd been crying.

—How did we end up here? I asked her.

—The Lord created us, she said without hesitation. Man and woman, He created them.

—Yes, I meant here in the music room.

My previous night's brush with death had left me weak and afraid. I heard some kids outside riding skateboards. The growl of rubber skateboard wheels resounded in my ears. Shadow barked. A FedEx truck stopped outside the Valenkemps' house. Somebody's stereo played "Time After Time" by Cyndi Lauper. Red welts showed on my wrists where my kidnappers had wrapped the duct tape. The whole world felt abrasive to me. I was starting to see the sharpness of things without the smoothing plane of religion to soften them.

—You hired my husband, Rachel said, to play keyboards for the church.

—Yes, that's right. We're grateful you all are here.

—Guess what? They were playing one of your old sermons on the radio last night.

—Well, isn't that nice? How did we sound?

—Very moving, pastor. I was in the bathtub when you came on. I listened to the whole sermon and by time you were done, I didn't realize the water had gotten so cold. I was trembling all over, like you are now. But I loved the sermon. You were preaching about second chances, how Christ will give us a second chance even when we don't feel deserving of one.

—Yes, if you're willing to believe in His greatness, you need not believe in the greatness in yourself. His grace is enough. Yes, I remember. Coming alive through the power and the grace of the Almighty. Nice to know we're still getting some air time. You said I was on last night? Lord, I wish I'd known. I'd have tuned in. Yes, cold water can do that to a naked body.

—What happened to your wrists?

—Oh, the marks. Those cuffs on my new tunic. Yes, I must be allergic.

—Sure you're all right? You're shaking again.

Rachel, if you're listening tonight, I'll have you know, sweetheart, the mountains would shake at your presence, but that certainly was *not* the kind of shaking I had going on in my legs. I wasn't falling in love with you. We barely knew each other then. I was afraid for my family. These men had come out of nowhere, dragged me out of bed, taken me to some warehouse outside Salterra, and they'd pointed guns at my face. My body shook from fear.

If y'all don't know already, Rachel's very beautiful, she has a beautiful soul, but she's had a hard time with the death of her husband, so let's not send messengers to fetch her from the rooftop, all right? Rachel, if you're taking a bath tonight, you keep bathing. I'm no King David.

HE CAME AS HIMSELF, WITH HIS FENDER RHODES

I was in the barn sniffing paint when your dad crashed into our lives. We called Watershed "the barn" before it became Watershed Church. Mom had tasked me with a roller, drip cloth, and an aluminum tray of fresh paint. I was supposed to do the first coat on the stage steps, Mars black. I wanted to see if I could get high. I inhaled several times. The paint did not produce the desired results. Several feet away at a foldout table, Mom typed on this gray adding machine which spun a roll of receipt paper. The numbers appeared in pale-purple ink.

—We're gonna come up short again, honey.

Mom was saying this to my dad when a guy startled us by dropping two heavy suitcases in the doorway. He was wearing a black suit. Mom's hands flew off the keys for an instant, as if she'd entered the wrong code. Her machine rattled. She looked at the guy and resumed typing.

My dad was in his office, behind the stage. If he heard the guy, he would have remained in his chair with his nose buried in his leather-bound Bible for several minutes. My parents employed the strategy of looking busy when someone showed up for an audition. Put the person on the defensive. —You make him feel like you're doing him a favor, my dad would say. So when it's time to discuss responsibilities and salary, you're one step ahead.

Actually, Mom *was* busy that day. We still had to come up with a way to cover renovation expenses on the barn. We'd put down the security deposit and first month's rent. And we'd celebrated with grape juice when the IRS approved our tax-exempt status. But I was an ignoramus back then. I thought "tax-exempt" meant you didn't have to pay the bills.

So in walks Fred with his suitcases and drops them on the floor in front of us like we're a couple of bellhops, and he's arrived at a hotel after a long ride and wants to check in.

First, Nelle, let me tell you, we were in need of Fred's services.

Since y'all live next door to Watershed, you have the easiest commute. But I don't envy you. Even if my TV here's covered in plexiglass and I'm walking around in a pair of green-padded socks. Even if my Converse wouldn't stay on my feet after they took away my shoelaces. It's nice to put some distance between myself and the Jesus freaks, no offense.

Before I realized how water can kill you, I enjoyed throwing bread crumbs at the ducks on Salterra Creek right there by Sal's BBQ with the old stream wheel out front. Nobody bothered me. At first, none of the folks my dad poached from New Foundations, his core membership, seemed to mind the Sunday drive up from San Antonio. It's only forty miles.

When it comes to handing out directions, my dad can get sesquipedalian. You like that word, Nelle? Sesquipedalian. Long-winded, tedious. I finally followed your suggestion and requested a dictionary. I got *Webster's*. And a few volumes of an expired *Encyclopaedia Britannica*. By "expired" I don't mean dead, only out-of-date. Anyway, ask my dad the best route to Watershed, he'll paint you a map, then he'll update you on the whole town.

He'll tell you which roads to take, which ones to avoid, who's burning their trash, who's not pruning their viburnum, who's suffering migraines so if you're coming at night you'll want to switch to lowbeams or turn off your headlights altogether, who's sleeping in the garage after falling off the wagon again. Who's drinking schnapps on the roof again. You heard him on the radio? It's embarrassing, Nelle. Somebody's got to stop giving him so much air time.

Our musicians hated the commute. They were hungover and tired from their Saturday night gigs. I guess that's how we lost our original piano player. My dad wouldn't pay him the extra gas money to make it worth his while.

Fred took a long look at our unfinished barn, the paint cans, the power tools, the ladder, the sawhorse, the balled fast-food wrappers on the floor. Probably trying to figure out what all he'd just walked into. —Saw in the paper y'all are looking for a piano player, he said.

—You got a piano chopped in half in those bags? My dad came forward wiping his hands with a rag that smelled of turpentine. The paint cans and drip cloths were piled behind Mom's desk. The chemical smell of fresh paint and turpentine masked whatever trace of horse manure or hay we hadn't been able to scrub off the floor.

—My name's Fred Valenkemp. I got a Fender Rhodes in one. He pointed to each suitcase. In the other, I got my effects pedals. Got a vocalizer, harmonizer, reharmonizer, a re-reharmonizer, and a Clavichord LCD-m5.

—You said Fender Rhodes?

A hitch of nostalgia crept into my dad's voice. Mom and I knew where this was going. Musicians snap together like toy magnets. Before you know it, they're in a jam session.

—Haven't seen one of those since my recording days. Zacharias glanced at Mom and me and smiled. —Y'all go about your business. Fred, back to my office. We'll talk.

IN THE BEGINNING: B'RUH-*SHEET*!

Let me set the record straight. I didn't get "diverted" to South Padre like my daughter claims. Before I called myself Zacharias, people called me Zach. I was a proud composer. I wrote jingles for Anheuser-Busch, Ford Motor Company, Remington Bank, Dodge, and various perfumes for women. I thought I was a big deal. Meanwhile, my soul sat hovering above the abyss, a formless void. My purpose in life? Cash weekly royalty checks I assumed would keep coming, head to the beach, haul towels and chairs, drag a cooler of beer.

Lather, rinse, repeat.

Problem is I'd drag my wife and young daughter as well. They'd watch seagulls claim our leftovers from lunch. They'd watch me drink beer. And more beer. Until the cooler was empty, and I was handing Lourna a wrinkled ten to go buy me another six pack, couldn't rise out of my beach chair. Why did Lourna put up with my behavior? Why didn't she leave me? Thank the Lord Elizabeth doesn't remember those days. I wasn't violent, but I was an ugly son-a-bitch. Folks, you do not want me to go back there. However, there's a lesson, if you'll hold on a second. And I am not ashamed to admit I drank a lot of beer.

And I had not found Jesus.

Which reminds me, folks, it's not too early to start planning our Thanksgiving Dinner. Last year we had a wonderful spread. Lourna's father did an excellent job with the table décor. Kids made those wonderful maple leaves. Everything tasted delicious. We regret the salmonella outbreak, but what can you do? One bad turkey spoils—wait, that's right, y'all cooked five. Praise Jesus. The generosity of this church. Amazing. I'll put a sign-up sheet on the table in the lobby. We'll get the temperatures right this year, I promise. Volunteers, we need you.

Shortly after my daughter Elizabeth was born, before I'd found Jesus, my brother died in a motorcycle accident. I took advantage of his untimely death to feel important and deserving if I got heavily drunk on Bohemia and expensive Panamanian Rum on weekends. I would make toasts to my brother at the beach. I would sob at sunsets.

The tributes weren't like my sermons. I'd lament the brevity of life, how you could die any second, which my brother did when his Willie G. Special hit a patch of black ice in Arizona one early spring morning, and he fell into the Grand Canyon. Nobody in my family knew Arizona had ice. We'd never left our hometown of San Antonio. Actually, since my wife's probably listening to this broadcast—Hi, honey, you still up?—I should point out, she always does, it wasn't the Grand Canyon per se but a large gulch near Flagstaff.

Rocks poked out of thin sheets of snow. The trucker who found my brother's body said he was lying there like a man wrapped in a black cloak among giant watermelon seeds.

Watermelon seeds are slippery.

That's not the point. Point is, I missed my brother. My bro. My guy. My hombre. *Mi hermano*. I don't speak Spanish but I like the way it sounds: *mi hermano*. Whatever Elizabeth may tell y'all about Fred winning me over with his keyboard wizardry, when he showed up at Watershed, I saw my brother.

I didn't see Fred. And not my brother exactly, but close enough. The black clothes, the cut over the eye, the lonesome-traveler-dragging-his-past-around-in-his-suitcases kind of look. You know what I'm talking about. I saw my brother lying in a patch of snow. I saw him get up and walk forward through the snow. I saw him step into our church. I saw his Harley waiting for him on stage, which Elizabeth hadn't finished painting, but never mind. I saw him straddle his Willie G. Special. I saw him kick-start the Beast in front of a live audience.

Only, the motorcycle had transformed into a Fender Rhodes.

Rocks, watermelon seeds. Willie G., Fender Rhodes. We can throw names around all night. When you dig beneath the surface, when you're struggling to make sense of death and rebirth and how it all fits together, what difference do a couple of brand names make?

In this part of the service, I'd normally take a moment.

I'd lower my head, pinch the top of my nose, close my eyes, and make small rotating movements with my shoulders to let you know I'm crying. After a few head shakes, I would actually cry. I can do that. Okay, I'm crying. I revisited South Padre. Hey, folks, admitting when your wrong? That's an important life skill, especially if you're a pastor who thinks of his congregation as his entire family. A pastor should cry in front of his family. A pastor *who is human* should admit fault in front of his family.

Maybe they don't they teach you those things in seminary, but where I come from, you can't expect to move people unless you yourself are moved.

And I am moved, so help me God.

So when Fred stepped into our barn and threw his suitcases down, I said to myself, Jesus has sent me a message. I am to treat this man like my brother. He will become my Brother-in-Christ. Excuse me? What's that? (Sorry, someone's shouting at us from behind the sound barrier.) I can't read your lips, man. You're saying everyone knows Arizona has ice?

Well, I didn't. Like I said, I'm from San Antonio.

SPIRITUALLY DISRUPTIVE:
HOW WE'RE NOT LIKE OTHER CHURCHES

—There's no formal audition, my dad probably said in his office. Play something for us.

While Fred went to build his keyboard, I spied on him from backstage. A dented scoop lit up the wrinkles in his shirt. His suit begged for some needlework. I saw a rip on his lapel. Leather boots. A short haircut made his ears stick out. He hadn't shaved. A tiny Band-Aid covered the tail of his right eyebrow.

Gold rings shimmered on his fingers, and a gold watch on his wrist. While he attached pedals and cables to his instrument, the jewelry on his hands mimicked the enticing, erratic triggering wobbles of a fisherman's spoon as it flashes under clear water.

I had no idea what musical furniture Fred was putting together, but the swift precision of his fingers as he plugged the gold-tipped cables into metal boxes—called four-channel mixers, I'd later learn—led me to realize he'd been playing the role of traveling musician for a long time. He effected the robotic fussiness of a seasoned troubadour. With my dad's band, he would embrace the thankless art of setting up and striking instruments before and after shows.

(Nelle, he made the cut, and I'll get back to the audition in a moment.)

Rarely would Fred talk during his stagecraft. He'd adjust microphones for the backup singers, he'd tape electrical cords to the stage, he'd line the drumkit platform with blue and pink striplights. One time he rigged a fog machine so Pastor Zacharias could jump on stage and sing with heavenly clouds rising up behind him like angel wings. Gag me, please.

Once Fred persuaded the church band to "go electric," Zacharias said he wanted to wire Watershed with some "most awesome Jesus Christ voltage." I'm not sure the band knew what that meant, but there was no going back to the days of acoustic folk. When Fred unpacked his machinery, Zacharias's face would light up with joy, then darken with worry.

Performing with synthesizers and amplified effects meant Zacharias would come to depend on Fred for the band's overall sound quality. Fred would arrive early and leave late. He didn't want anybody to learn how to assemble his gear. Eventually he brought his own mixing board, and he wouldn't let anyone touch the dials. If he ever failed to show up for a rehearsal or service, my dad and the Praise Team would have freaked. They still owned their acoustic instruments, but it had been so long since they'd touched the old songs. They'd struggle. Like when Dylan went electric at Newport, backpedaled after the boos, and had to ask the crowd, "Anybody have an E harmonica? An E harmonica, anybody! Just throw them all up."

Other churches in Salterra offered both traditional and contemporary services at different times on Sundays. Watershed did not. Shortly after Fred's arrival, we went all contemporary, all the time. It seemed to work. More people attended. Parents brought their kids to the rocking music school, and there'd be the sweet girl (me) passing out brochures, and why don't y'all stick around for the music and donuts and coffee? It's gonna be so much fun!

Parents who had no intention of joining a church found themselves surrounded by hand-clapping worshipers simply because they'd enrolled their kids in one of the private or group music lessons offered by Freedom Keys. Listen to my dad talk on the radio, and you'd think it was God's plan all along, as if God handpicked Fred and Rachel to help him create Freedom Keys as his sole means of delivering the financial gains visited upon Watershed.

My dad's services were carefully scripted. Going off script was part of the script, especially during sermons. It took the spectacle of Fred's creative improvising to complement the wild sermonizing of Pastor Zacharias, whose idea of religious entertainment required disruptive, childlike behavior. Falling off the stage, lying on the floor, pretending his microphone didn't work, using props like a paper shredder and a children's picture book to attack Charles Darwin's *On the Origin of Species by Means of Natural Selection, or the Preservation of Favoured Races in the Struggle for Life.*

—We have all these pieces of paper, see?

He threw the confetti at his congregants seated in the front row, interrupted himself to apologize to the custodian (me) who would have to vacuum the mess after the service, then held up a copy of *Make Way for Ducklings.*

—And we're supposed to believe all these random scraps of paper turned into this book? This beautifully designed *book*? These shreds of paper happened to come together, to make words and pictures? All this happened *without* an Author?

Plus, you gotta be disruptive if you're denouncing Satan and calling upon the Holy Spirit to work miracles for your fellow Brothers and Sisters in Christ.

You gotta hold the microphone so close to your mouth it looks like you're gonna swallow the ball head. At times you gotta speak hardly above a whisper and at other times you gotta scream. Sometimes you need to chant in a rhythmic monotone like an auctioneer. Other times you need to vary your intonation to the extreme and let the spit fly:

—Take away the cancer, Lord.

—Give him that job in the name of Jesus, Amen.

—Heal his fractured hip, Father God, Hallelujah.

—Give her that promotion she's been praying for, Sweet Jesus.

—Let him rise *up* out of that wheelchair and walk again in the Name of Jesus!

—Get rid of the AIDS from her body, Lord. Get it out of there.

Actually, he probably never mentioned AIDS. Calling to someone in his congregation with AIDS or HIV would've sent the frightened sheep stampeding through the exit doors. For someone like my dad, AIDS signified the very "pestilence" of the Second Coming.

BRIEF INTERLUDE OF WHAT HE CANNOT FORGIVE

I won't do it, folks. I *can't* do it. I will never forgive Ozzie Osbourne for urinating on the Alamo. I'm sorry. Even if it wasn't technically the Alamo but that sixty-foot Cenotaph directly across from the sacred fort where those brave men gave their lives. When you grow up, the way I do, when you come to JESUS, the way I have, some things you can never forgive.

BACK TO THE DEVIL IN THE BLACK SUIT

For his audition, Fred finished plugging in his plugs, testing out the pads on his keyboard. He was already a little sweaty and had a certain smell, but Zacharias did not seem to notice. Fred patted his hair into place and asked Zacharias what he should play.

—Oh, I don't know, my dad said. How about "Amazing Grace"?

—Dad, I said. Everybody knows that one. Give him something harder to play.

—"Amazing Grace in G," my dad said.

I rolled my eyes. Easiest key in the world.

All three of us sat on stage while Fred played "Amazing Grace" at a tasteful tempo in waltz time. I'm no prodigy, but I knew good hymn-playing when I heard it. Obviously Fred wanted us to like him right away, but why didn't Zacharias at least make him play a harder song? He could've called for "Jesus, I'll Never Forget," or "Say the Name." On the last verse of "Amazing Grace," Zacharias sang along, harmonizing with Fred's electric-organ chords, and somehow near the end Fred knew when to drop off to let Zacharias sing the "Amazing" part solo, and Fred returned with a gentle arpeggio on the final "Grace."

While Zacharias and Mom were still clapping, Fred said he would now like to play one of his own compositions, a "concerto," he called it, although at first it didn't sound like a concerto. It didn't sound like any music I'd ever heard. Fred switched on a backing track, and through the speakers beneath his keyboard came the sweep of strings, a random swelling of sound, like an orchestra noodling around before the conductor comes on stage.

Gradually the strings produced a pattern of five or six different parts (later, Fred would call this the "fugue" section), and while the different melodies collided, separated, and rejoined, Fred slammed his hands into the upper register of his keyboard, laying on several quick schizophrenic chords. Even stranger, the middle of his concerto had a hole in it, a donut hole of silence we had to sit through, like punished students, Fred shaking his head *no* to tell us the piece wasn't over, and when the strings came back on it was the same weird orchestral swelling, and I wondered, God, how long is this going to last? His fingers worked down in the lower register, his foot hit another pedal to end the fugue, and his playing steered us into a vamp, a single phrase that snaked around in the bass, which boomed in the barn's warped floorboards, traveled through our feet, and hummed in our spines. For three, four, five seconds. Fred stomped the pedals, swept his hands into the treble, and crashed them against the keys in double octaves to the end.

Without a word, he nodded and packed up his gear.

I'd never heard the barn so quiet. Outside the trees sighed and rasped in the breeze. The window units ticked. They say Lucifer's demons sing better in hell than all the angels in heaven combined, and I thought, that's what Fred did, for those ten or fifteen minutes, he'd transformed our barn into the original pandemonium, all the demons singing together in hell in perfect harmony. My dad stood and clapped and shouted his "bravo!" Then his face darkened.

—Truth is, he said. We can't pay you much. Not at first.

—That's all right. I don't need a lot.

—You deserve more. All that *equipment*?

—I don't have to use them.

—You wanted by the law?

—No, sir. I'm here with my wife and daughter. We lived in New York. Then Houston. Trying to make it as a musician. I got lost along the way.

—You moved a lot of heavy furniture, am I right?

My dad and Fred laughed, as if they shared a special history.

—Or you dog-walked for the rich ladies on the Upper East Side, my dad said. Doesn't matter. I'll tell you why you didn't make it.

I knew where my dad was going. Fred won over Pastor Zacharias Hembrey not by accepting a low-to-nonexistent salary but by calling upon my dad's particular need, urgent need, to preach the Word to a fellow Brother-in-Christ. For reasons I can't explain, my dad needed Fred to remind him of his Purpose in Life.

—You didn't *make* it in the commercial life, Zacharias continued, because your heart hadn't turned to Jesus. And it's a blessing you failed. God has greater plans for you, my friend. His plans go beyond anything you could ever imagine. See, I was like you. I wanted commercial success. I got it. I wanted more. I searched and searched all up and down the coast for the right answers, but in this world, you'll only find trouble.

—"Have no fear, for I have overcome the world."

—Good. You know your scripture. If you join us, we will welcome you. This will be your home. Zacharias extended his hand, and Fred shook it. —Y'all will never be alone.

THAT'S HOW GOD WORKS IN US

If we can get back to the music room, I was talking about the morning Rachel found me trembling and how I realized something troubled Rachel, too. The faded Cleopatra marks. Normally in this part of the service, I'd toss out an anecdote, something to take the trouble off her mind. If she cracks a smile, if she shows only a glimmer, you'll win her over with Hope. Hope is what you see in her before she sees it in herself.

That's the Holy Spirit, how God works in us.

—You wouldn't believe, I said after she helped me off the floor and noticed my shaking legs. I'd get so nervous as a kid, I told her. I'd crap in my pants.

—What? Rachel stepped back, horrified. Her hand went to her mouth again.

—Walking home from school because I'd get so nervous?

—Why?

No glimmer yet, but y'all have patience.

—Walking home from football practice, or maybe I only *thought* I'd taken a crap, and my father always said dirty kids who shit themselves go straight to hell.

—That's awful. Rachel shook her head, looked at the floor, blinked away tears.

—Wait. That's not how it was supposed to go. I'm sorry.

My eyes found a poster on the wall, of Jesus holding the Lamb, a copy of a "Jesus, Lamb of God" painting, and I hummed to myself:

Rachel had a big, big smile,
Big, big smile, big, big smile.
Rachel had a big, big smile
Her teeth were white as snow.
And everywhere that Rachel went
The men were sure to go!

—It's not that, she said. She wiped her face.

Her wrists were thin but her hands were strong, her nails cut short, no polish. When she spoke, a rose formed at the base of her throat, a pink rush of blood that widened and vanished under her skin like a hillside cloud-shadow beneath the green. All right, let's get the rest of her description out of the way: She wore a dark green V-neck sweater. Also, a modest shin-length skirt or wrap of light-brown cotton. Beige dress shoes without socks, or else with no-show socks, showing her ankles. Which were perfectly fine, beautiful ankles.

I'm only describing her ankles so y'all can walk her across the room.

Rachel left me and went to the suitcase with her husband's Fender beside the conga drums, and she kept going and finally sat on the piano bench.

—What's the matter, Rachel? You can talk to me.

By this time I must have been leaning against the desk, one of those teacher desks with a hand-crank pencil sharpener bolted to the surface. My backside found the sharpener. A dull metal edge pushed into the hip pocket of my blue jeans.

—My father never said that about dirty kids.

—Pastor, it's all right. You don't have to try so hard.

—That's what my daughter says. I'd hoped my need to sound clever wouldn't rub off on her. There's smart and there's smart. The "Hembrey" smart murders you at job interviews.

—Have you ministered all your adult life?

—Did a stint in advertising. Our daughters are the same age.

—Thirteen.

—Never thought I'd father a teenager. You ready?

Rachel shook her head. Parenting wasn't what was bothering her.

—Yeah, I said. Me, neither.

She put her hands on the edge of the piano bench. Her fingertips graced the wood the way a platform diver swipes the concrete edge before she falls into a routine of twisting somersaults. The space between her thumbs and index fingers formed two hollow inverted triangles.

She was a pianist, yes. The musculature of the hands, the fingernails—clipped, not bitten. A *classical* pianist, turned out. Bach, Mozart, Beethoven, Brahms. She knew them. And I'm willing to bet Fred Valenkemp did not. Without his effects, he probably lacked his wife's talent at the keys. (Rachel, what your husband did was sinful, leaving you and Nelle behind.)

But he died, so I guess we'll never know for sure.

Herbie Hancock was a champion of the Fender Rhodes. I forgive him for being a Buddhist. If he were a Muslim, I'd still say he's awesome. I don't agree with Keith Jarrett that electronic keyboards are toys and what can you do with toys besides have fun?

What's wrong with having fun? They don't call it "working music," or "struggling music," or "slaving music." They call it *"playing music."* It's play.

Rachel kept her back to the Baldwin Hamilton, which unbeknownst to us stood jam packed with premium cocaine. Imagine her seated before a wooden box with thousands of dollars' worth of drugs inside? Not knowing a thing? Well, lucky for me, Rachel didn't attempt to play. —I came here, she said, to warn you about Fred.

—My Brother-in-Christ? What's up?

—Your Brother-in-Christ is a little possessive.

—No kidding. Haven't seen it. (I had. His attention on the equipment. Not letting anyone help him run the cables or plug in the amplifiers. I didn't want to hurt her feelings.)

—We have him on medication.

—You're not a drug dealer, are you?

A dart shot through my chest. I recalled my night in the warehouse—roaches, gunpowder, fruit flies—and my head became a Rayleigh-Taylor instability. My skull overheated like a lava lamp with my brain blended into ascending blobs of wax.

Rachel said she was a sales rep for a pharmaceutical company. She didn't say which, but later I found out it was McKesson. (Sorry, Rachel. Not sure if you wanted me to spill those beans. Nothing wrong with big-pharma, though, in my humble opinion.)

—So, she said. In a way, I *am* a drug dealer.

Rachel shot up off the bench and went for her purse behind me on the desk. What had she been doing at the desk? While she dug around, I smelled fresh-cut grass and something evergreen, maybe rosemary, but none of the perfumes I'd written ridiculous melodies for all those years ago. In her palm, she held a single dice, ten-sided, only slightly larger than your standard dice. The "six" side flipped open. Out rolled an oval blue pill.

—Take this.

—Oh, no thanks. I don't partake.

—It'll calm you down.

—I've sworn off chemicals. Gotta keep my body pure for Jesus.

Nothing I said came out right, and yet to this day I can assure you we were having a conversation in plain English. We understood each other.

After she popped the pill and gulped it dry, I eased my hip off the pencil sharpener and cleared my throat. Over the next several minutes, while she explained how her husband Fred "bonds" with people

(—You think he's being polite. He's not, he's obsessing. He *obsesses* over me.), while I listened to her talk, the creases around her mouth and at the corners of her eyes vanished, the muscles in her shoulders slackened, and I thought how if my daughter could feel this way for an instant, I would resign as Pastor of Watershed Church, effective immediately. The decision would be a difficult one, but I would truly believe my presence at Home with Elizabeth would be what's best for my family.

I opened up to Rachel about our struggle with my daughter's mental health, and how Jesus hadn't shown us, "us" meaning me and Lourna, how to talk to Elizabeth.

—Why don't you listen to what *she* has to say? Rachel said.

—I understand. Don't get me wrong. You wanna know what she says?

(This was gonna be a gamble, I thought. Usually I'm the one listening, offering comfort, a reassuring hug or pat on the back, not shocking people with false accusations.) —She says your husband is Satan and he'll ruin our lives.

Finally Rachel laughed. I don't know if it was me or the pill. I hoped it was me. I laughed, too, and for the first time that morning, I felt like a normal everyday prophet again.

KEEPING HIS OPEN MIND CLOSED

There's a picture of me at our house in San Antonio, I'm two or three, and my dad's carrying me on his back. My chubby legs bounce from the sling of an infant carrier strapped to his shoulders. Judging by the fat rolls on my legs, the chunk in my cheeks, my double chin, I'm a heavy sack of weight. But when I look at the picture now, I only think Zach has no idea how much I'll weigh on him in the future. He has no idea of the real burden I'll become.

In the picture, he's holding a garden hose with the nozzle set to "shower" mode. A vegetable garden wrapped in chicken wire spreads behind us and fills the rest of the frame: tomatoes, green beans, squash, cucumbers, bell peppers. My infant eyes are fixed on the hose. When I'm older, I'll slide the nozzle to "jet" mode. I'll shove the hose into the dirt and turn on the water to blast a subterranean ant colony into the stratosphere. Soldier ants and baby ants and mother ants will all ride my tsunami over the curb into the street, where they'll dry out in the sun. When I'm older, I'll take pleasure in drowning insects.

In the photo, my dad's standing there about to water the garden, lowering his shower wand to one of the mounds beneath a tomato plant. I can almost see the mulch turning light brown to black. I can almost see the dirt sponge up the water. Maybe I squeal and kick my feet against his sides like I'm riding horsey. When I fall asleep, he'll feel my forehead settle against the back of his neck. My legs will flex and go limp. I can smell the bug spray and suntan lotion smeared over our skin. I can smell the sweat on his neck as I nuzzle against him.

My father always carried two kinds of sweat: booze sweat, of which I was terrified, and yardwork sweat, which I always craved, a pleasant smell, the outdoor summer smell of cut grass, rich soil, and his pine aftershave that always said dad. Unfortunately, as I grew older, he worked less in the yard and more in his office, writing jingles for companies that paid him too much, and then the booze sweat replaced the yardwork sweat, and I would stop hoping for the chance to ride on his shoulders or walk beside him. I'd stop hoping for our summer garden.

It's possible our garden didn't exist much beyond the day the photo was taken. If I look closely, I can see the tips of the tomato leaves turning brown. I can see the root hairs poking through the soil where mulch should've been added. I can see the smile stitched into my father's face, a smile that says he's found a lucky surprise, a garden full of vegetables he forgot he planted. He's surprised anything came up at all, and why don't we pose here with the garden hose to make it look like this whole thing arrived by design? By summer's end, the garden, untouched by his hands, will shrivel into dead kindling, overrun by weeds. The sacks of rotten tomatoes will hang on the vines like popped balloons after a birthday party.

No surprise, our yard in Salterra lacks the space and sunlight for a garden. Plus, there's no depth to the soil. No depth at all. Shadow digs holes everywhere, but after pawing for just a few moments, she clicks her nails against limestone. Each time she digs, she doesn't remember her claws will hit limestone, the sound makes my skin crawl, and I grab her collar and yank her back to the porch. She sniffs my hands, inhales the smell of brisket and beans from dinner lingering on my fingers, and then she sinks down beside me and slurps the rain out of a tipped-over flower pot, or she licks the wet stem of a dandelion weed.

Sensing my loneliness, Zach comes out with his dinner and sits behind me in a lawn chair. He's carrying his brisket and corn on one of those cheap Dixie plates with a green triangle drawn like a child's drawing of a Christmas tree, the word "joy" written in sloppy red cursive letters. It's summer again, so I don't have to guess he has bought a ton of these plates wholesale. We'll be using and reusing them until December, when he'll take the bulk of the plates to Watershed for the annual Christmas Dinner. So many meals riding on a cheap Dixie plate, so many mouths to feed in the name of Christ Jesus. They'd all starve without him, he'll say.

—It's a glorious evening, he says, a lilt in his voice.

—It's going to rain, I reply. The mosquitos are out.

—You hate it here, don't you?

—You read my mind. You must be a genius.

—Come on, Liz. It's not so bad. Why don't you invite Grant over?

Grant was a kid my age who sat in front of us at New Foundations. A decent kid, he had freckles on his chin and long sideburns, and he talked nonstop about his favorite rock band. He'd go on about Rick Allen, the one-armed drummer of Def Leppard, as if I shared his enthusiasm. But he was nicer than most boys. Not like the jerks who hid under the bleachers during Athletics to look up our wind shorts. One time I got sent to the principal's office for throwing pea gravel at a boy who snapped pictures at us with his portable Kodak.

—You only want me to call Grant, I told my dad, so you can talk his parents into joining our church. You're still mad they didn't follow us out here to Hell-terra.

—That's not true. I want you to have friends. I want you to have fun.

He tossed an acorn at the fence. Shadow lifted her head but didn't chase it.

—How can I have fun? There's nothing to *do* here.

—You could have Nelle over. Isn't it nice to have a neighbor your age? She's only a few blocks down. Y'all could ride bikes together. Y'all could hang out.

—I hang out with Nelle at her house. I wouldn't want her here. It's too embarrassing.

—What do y'all do at Nelle's house?

—Nothing. Her dad has a cool music studio.

—So I've heard. How's Fred?

—I don't know. He's weird. Nelle says he stays up all night.

—He's an adult. He's free to do what he wants.

—What if he's chopping up people and stuffing their body parts in his suitcases?

—What have you been watching?

—Nothing.

I went into the yard and pulled a clump of dirt from one of Shadow's holes. The dirt was dry and chalky, held together with root hairs. I rubbed some of the dirt between my fingers and dropped it back into the hole. —We should start a garden.

—We'd have to cut back those tree limbs, build a raised bed, a fence. Garden takes work. Weeding, mulching, fertilizing. You willing to put in the work?

—Before you became a servant of God, we used to do stuff together.

—I'm still your father. We can do stuff. I just can't go back to what I was before. The money, the boredom. Remember how miserable I made everyone? I was in a dark place.

—You call this bright? We don't have even enough light for a decent garden.

—Salterra was the right move. There was too much corruption at New Foundations. I couldn't trust the leaders anymore. Out here, we know everyone. Our congregants are family. When the head is rotten, Liz, you can't ride the tail. You have to toss out the whole body.

—Or stuff it in a suitcase. (I smiled.)

Zach rolled his shoulders, and a bone in his neck popped.

—We can make this work, he said. Keep an open mind.

THE LIGHTS ARE OFF BUT SOMEONE'S HOME

Something tells me Elizabeth had a little help with her last letter. Her words flowed like the River Jordan, milk and honey on the other side, and from *her* side, from her perspective, she barely mentioned Nelle. Is it possible the ruse is up? She's no longer pretending Nelle's her target audience? One of the nurses at Warm Springs must have helped her.

I'm sorry, Liz. We failed to connect. I never built you the garden you wanted. I was too busy growing my flock. We needed tithes, many tithes, before we could hang out in the back yard and talk about how God germinates seeds according to His Design.

My daughter's repetition is deliberate, not a sign of amnesia, not a side effect of her medication. Not a sign of parental neglect. The good doctors would've warned us about potential memory loss. These new drugs are more effective than the neuro-twisting pharmaceutical garbage Fred Valenkemp was ingesting the night he died. I remember the garden. It's no secret. Summers in Texas require constant watering to maintain a healthy crop. I remember the tomatoes, the inedible eggplant, the cucumbers that sucked up my hose water. The photo makes gardening look like a breeze. Was I supposed to stand outside watering all day?

I installed a soaker hose on a timer, but the soaker never worked, never hit the sweet spots, that greedy soil at the root base beneath the low branches. It's not practical for a working man to water his garden morning, noon, and night, and I'll tell you what else is not practical: maintaining any semblance of order and calm when you've got criminals (and I'm talking about the Alejandro Brothers and their crew) hiding their shrink-wrapped bricks of cocaine behind the walls of a House of the Lord. It's hard to keep an open mind about drug lords.

But if y'all want, I'll get down on my knees and pray for these sinners, who've brought a whole new level of corruption into my growing flock. That's right. I haven't seen the men who work for the Alejandro Brothers. Haven't seen their faces. I assume they're attending my church. Keeping an eye on things. Making sure nobody slips up.

Forgive me if in my sermons I avoid any mention of honesty and instead focus on servitude, blind obedience. I fear these new lords, I wish them gone, and yet I obey them.

Our tomato plants were very sensitive not only to sunlight but to the touch of human hands. Elizabeth and I left marks on the stems, light-green scratches, when we planted them. I don't remember her habit of drowning insects, but if she says it happened, I'm willing to believe her. One time she picked up two cicada shells, brown and brittle, and attached them to her earlobes. —Mom, look at my new earrings.

Lourna screamed. She thought the carapaces dangling from her daughter's ears were alive. Elizabeth took them off and crushed them in her hands, and she blew the exoskeleton dust onto the kitchen tile. She wanted to show her mother the shells were harmless, and Lourna just wanted a daughter who didn't pick up dead things and wear them like jewelry.

—Don't beetles carry E. coli? Lourna said.

—They're not beetles, Mom. They're cicadas.

For Halloween we dressed her up in a frog costume. A ball of green fur with plastic Kermit eyes on the top of her head. She filled her pockets not with candy but with plastic spider rings and rubber snakes and dragonflies. A frog who likes to drown her meals before she eats them. Liz, you were also obsessed with insect tunnels. The mail-order ant farm. The science project at school. The massive colony behind the plexiglass wall at the zoo. You could stand there for hours watching ants carry the white sacks of their eggs down the steep tunnels.

—Keep an open mind? she said that evening in the yard, when she'd told me she wanted to build another garden together. —What's that mean? It sounds to me like you're okay with living this stupid naïve life where you ignore all the trouble around you.

—I'm not ignoring them, I said. I'm not naïve. Faith has reformed me.

Elizabeth rolled her eyes, got up, and went to the gate. I asked her where she was going. She said she wanted to take a walk. —A walk? I said, alarmed. It's almost dark.

—It's not dark yet.

—It will be soon.

—So take a flashlight. Wow, since when are you afraid of the dark?

—I'm not. It's just late, I'm not sure.

—What is it about this place? Why did you bring us here? We used to take walks at night all the time in San Antonio? I wish we hadn't moved. I hate it here.

—It's not so bad.

—There's nothing to do. We can't even take a walk.

—Okay, we're walking. Let's go.

Right then, folks, I wanted to tell her exactly who we were dealing with: drug lords with machine guns. I wanted to lift her into my arms, yell at Lourna to start up the car, drive my family out of there, never to set foot in Salterra again. I also knew that if we ran, they'd find us, and it wasn't hard to imagine the kind of damage these men did to people who ran. Besides, I had a moral responsibility. My congregants needed me. We had souls to save, including my daughter's. If I preached the Word, I believed we'd come out okay.

I went inside and grabbed the leash off the nail I'd hammered into the frame of the back door, figuring if we were going to walk at night, we'd better take the dog, not that I put any faith in Shadow's ability to defend us against kidnappers with AK-47s.

Liz took the leash and we went down the rutted road past the church. The lights were off at Watershed. Hallelujah. Nobody was in there digging holes in our walls. Nobody was in there hollowing out our piano. Not yet. Maybe after a walk I would actually get some sleep.

Christmas lights hung in the windows of Annie's Antiques on Main. The lights left a glaze on the sidewalk's gray pavement. I reminded myself which shops needed our brochures. Which business owners could use a follow-up. My obsession with growing the church was like a summer lightning bug that flickered in and out of my consciousness but never really stopped flying. I thought about whether the Alejandros would contact me again. Only if I screwed up. I mustn't screw up. I thought about what I'd wear for my next sermon, whether to splurge on a new suit, whether Fred would show up for the service. Fred's contribution to the band was almost too good to be true. I worried we'd lose him to some record producer, some touring Broadway musical, a rock opera. He'd split, and I'd have to scramble for another keyboardist.

—Besides raising Fred's pay, I asked Elizabeth, how can we keep him with us?

—Why do you want to keep him with us?

Liz took Shadow to urinate at her favorite spot behind a pecan tree. I stood between my daughter and Main, thinking if the Alejandros decided to pull a drive-by, at least I'd be able to shove her out of the way before their first round hit me in the back. I'd scream *Run!* like they do in the movies when the guy's body convulses and smokes with bullets, T-shirt ripping open and filling with blood, and somehow the guy's still able to talk.

> *Run away, my child,*
> *You are free.*
> *You will never be*
> *Punished for the sins*
> *Of your father…*

Another annoying jingle had popped into my ears. These spontaneous earworms, echoes of my former life, mocked me in moments of panic and never wanted to quit. Shadow had finished her business and was sniffing among the leaves, nosing the stiff carcass of a squirrel.

—Come on, I said, grabbing her leash. Let's go home.

—Go home? Elizabeth said. You mean San Antonio?

—Nice try. I mean our new home. Listen, I have to confess something. I've been lying to myself about being a successful pastor. I'm worried everyone can see through the lie.

—That isn't lying, she said. That's faking it until you make it.

—You're too mature for your age. You know that? What if I don't make it?

—If Jesus doesn't want you to become a pastor, you'll do something else.

—Hey, how's the Fall Drive coming along? (Thinking a little responsibility might snap her out of her funk, I'd put Elizabeth in charge of helping our congregants collect gently worn clothing for our annual drive.) —Those ladies giving you any trouble with the bins?

—They're all right.

—What else is going on?

—Nothing.

—Come on, Liz. We used to talk. We can't be friends again if you don't open up.

She shrugged. —Who said I wanted to be friends with you?

—I thought, when you said we used to do stuff together.

Her silence meant she was still angry at me. She missed her friends in San Antonio, Grant from New Foundations, the kid with the freckles and long sideburns. She missed the house, her old room. I'd taken these things away from her, and she'd be angry at me for the rest of her life. It's depressing when you think how much time and love and nurturing you pour into your child, only to witness her become a teenager, walled up behind her hormones, indifference, confusion, anger. You try to crack the wall, praying a sliver of light breaks through.

We stood in the dark, and I hadn't brought a flashlight.

When we turned the corner, Elizabeth grabbed a handful of acorns off the sidewalk and hurled them over the road. The nuts clicked against the gravel like change falling out of your pocket. Shadow growled at something, and I tugged on her leash and whispered for her to hush, and I choked up on the leash. Elizabeth asked me who was at the church tonight.

—What? I looked up the road. The lights were on inside. No cars in the cul-de-sac. I imagined power drills piercing the stage. Electric saws cutting into drywall.

—Oh, probably Bailey, I said. He was going to test out the security system. Which would have made sense except I'd relieved Bailey, our volunteer night watchman, of his duties the day after my encounter with Lester and his thugs. They'd made it clear to me the Alejandro Brothers didn't want anyone in the church at night. A gust of wind blew more acorns out of the trees. A peel of thunder cracked in the distance. —Here comes your rain, I said. Let's go home.

—Maybe someone broke in, Elizabeth said. We should check it out.

—No, I said, and I put my arm around her shoulder, steering her towards our house. Bailey doesn't want anyone coming in. He needs it quiet for the system test.

Unlike Watershed, full of illegal activity that night, all was quiet at our house, not a single light on inside. The darkness meant Lourna was having another migraine.

I DID HEAR THEM TALKING IN THE GARAGE

Dear Nelle, if everything unfolds according to God's plan, if all is seen and heard and predicated on God's initial act or acts for the rest of humanity—like, what's the point?

You told me not to use "humanity" when writing, but this isn't some stupid essay for school. I'm trying to show what a hypocrite my dad was and *is* because after he met with Rachel in the music room, he returned to his old ways!

Zacharias had a long talk with ~~Mom~~. Sorry, I mean "Lourna" (I could hear them talking in the garage), and the next thing I knew, we were headed to South Padre Island. That's right. The same beach he'd sworn never to revisit.

When Zacharias says how he "thanks the Lord" Elizabeth doesn't remember those days? When Zacharias preaches about how he was so unworthy of our love and was a such-and-such? Hello, Dad? I'm ~~write~~ right here. I remember. (I'm so mad I can't spell. Sometimes when I think about him, it's like I'm shouting inside my own echo chamber.) Sorry, Nelle. Minor detour. I'll skip the boring drive. You probably don't want to hear about it anyway. Here's the major setback. He'll probably tell you it never happened:

The sun had set and the seagulls consumed the last of our stale hot dog buns and the crumbs of our potato chips. The cooler nestled beside him in the sand. A cold wind came down from Nova Scotia. Honestly, Nelle, I looked up "Nova Scotia" in *Webster's* and it sounded like a cold place. Colder than "Arizona," where my uncle died, so I'll go with Canada:

The cold Nova Scotia wind came down and blew the sand into Zacharias's face, stinging his eyes, and the same terrible wind swept over the face of the waters. And at this point, I feel like calling him just

"Zach." Did you ever call your father "Fred"? I don't believe my dad deserves his religious name anymore. At least not in my account.

Sorry, back to the story:

And then there was light. Zach built a bonfire on the beach with driftwood, half of somebody's discarded headboard, and liquid propane he'd brought himself. After he got the fire roaring, he wanted us to stay. —Honey, Lourna said to him. It's getting late.

—Seriously, Dad? (I was pissed.) —You're gonna force us to stand here while you drink and make stupid toasts to some uncle I never met?

Zach took off his T-shirt, stumbled backwards, ran towards the fire, and beat his chest. He'd had twelve beers. (The next morning Lourna was terrified we'd lose our deposit for the cleaning fee. She made me collect the dented cans off the beach and throw them away.)

—Yeah, I see the fire, Zach. Great. Now what?

—Now we enjoy the fire. Come on, don't hold back.

—I'm not holding back. I'm angry. You're acting like a child.

Zach smiled at me and reached into the cooler for another can of beer. I'm sure he chalked up my anger to teenage rebellion, but with his drinking and his antics by the fire, what did I have to rebel against? The power dynamics of our family, his leadership, which I liked to test but also took for granted, had shifted before my eyes, and I could feel us getting swept away. I was angry but also scared. He offered me a beer, and I slapped it out of his hand.

—This is stupid, I said. I don't even like beer. I want to go home.

WHY HE TRADED JESUS FOR TWELVE COLD BEERS

Folks, I don't know why she's inventing this tale, but I can explain the beers. Need I explain the beers? Guess so, when you consider Elizabeth's letter to Nelle. Elizabeth got it all wrong.

I realize she's my daughter, but she's crazy. This is the same person who swears she killed my keyboard player, Fred Valenkemp. Same child currently under psychiatric care at Warm Springs in San Antonio.

Same little raconteur who suffers aquaphobia, paranoia, major depression, generalized anxiety disorder. Who has shown signs of wrist-cutting, wound excoriation, and who exhibits a whole bunch of other sinfulness I can't get into on account of doctor-patient privilege.

Yes, I'm following Rachel's advice. I'm listening to my daughter. We're working on our problems. Although at this point in our dueling stories I'd hardly call her a reliable narrator, and now can I please explain about the beers and why I broke eight years of sobriety?

Minor setback.

You'll recall the guy I mentioned earlier, Lester Hargreve. Not a nice character. Lester and I knew each other from my South Padre days when I still had the royalty checks rolling in and too much free time on my hands and before I'd put Jesus at the Center. Lester owned a bar called Bait & Wait for the luckless fishermen who limped off the wharf every August with empty buckets, sunburned necks, and parched throats. Men who ponied up for a couple of beers and a chance to tell their story about the One That Got Away.

—It's why they call it "fishing," Lester would say. Not "catching."

Bait & Wait served only Mexican beer. Corona, Tecate, Negro Modelo, Bohemia.

Eight years of sobriety gone after Jesus rescued me from one night of pure terror. Guess I still needed to hear the pop of a cold bottle uncapped. Needed to taste the nice froth of a Bohemia sizzling up over its gold tinfoil. Back then, Lester sold me Bohemias, and I'd sneak shots of Panamanian Kaniché rum under the bar while Lourna and Elizabeth splashed in the ocean. I kept the good stuff in my backpack to avoid offending the patrons and Lester himself, who drank only from the country he served. By which I mean he "served" Mexican beers, and later, after his bar in Salterra failed, he "served" the Alejandro Brothers, Mexicans.

He and I were never friends. Okay, bar buddies. I don't remember what we talked about. Probably guns and war and hunting lions, Hemingway stuff. Most Bait & Wait patrons were ex-military. I don't think Lester was ex-military, but he owned guns.

I don't own guns. Nor am I about to trample on the Second Amendment rights of my fellow congregants. For the record, when we first moved to Salterra, Sheriff Lufkin told my wife that with a gun-ownership rate hovering at ninety-four percent, all cleared and registered, we might as well consider our neighborhood a well-regulated militia. I don't know if the sheriff meant to comfort or terrify Lourna with that comment, but I found myself smiling at my neighbors more often and calling up the parents of Elizabeth's friends, before she went over there, to ask if they had a gun in the house and did they keep it in a safe and did they store the ammo in a separate location such as a closet or up on a high shelf. I got mixed responses.

Before we moved to Salterra, the land of Guns and Gospel, I drank at Bait & Wait in South Padre, and I guess we all waited and waited. Until Hurricane Alicia kissed the Gulf Coast. We evacuated. Alicia flooded Lester's bar. Left him jobless for a spell.

How Lester bummed his way to Salterra is anybody's guess. When you're all washed up and too broke to buy a boat, only way to go is west. Every town in our county has at least one bar, and there's always plenty of Gospel. Somehow Lester found one of my "Put the Fun Back in Worship" pamphlets. Don't know if he liked my sermon. At the time, I was preaching out of a conference room at the Fair Weather Inn, one of those cheap by-hour spaces with harsh fluorescent lights and carpet that smells of mildew and continental breakfast. Lourna and I needed to raise more cash to renovate the barn.

—Howdy, stranger, he said to me.

GET TO THE POINT, ZACH

Nelle, we already know Lester Hargreve opened a bar in Salterra called Inferno. The name itself suggests Zach and Lester were closer than Zach admits. What's the point?

Zach went eight years without drinking. Now he's stalling, throwing his plot into reverse. "Minor setback"? Try major. He doesn't want me to say what happened at the beach.

Honestly, though, you think Zach was kidnapped?

Don't listen to him. He wouldn't have gone back to Lester's home turf *after* Lester kidnapped him. That makes no sense. You think he'd want to relive his drinking days with Lester over twelve beers? Yes, twelve, I counted them the following morning, and I know our English teacher would say I need to elaborate on the symbolism of the twelve beers and twelve apostles, as if my dad's decision to opt for the cheap cans instead of golden Bohemia represented some kind of lasting moral imprint, but honestly I'm too upset to analyze his behavior.

You think he'd return with his wife and daughter to the Isle of Perdition if Lester had actually threatened him? Zach would have got down on his knees for Lester to change his ways, prayed for him to come to Jesus, welcomed him home to Watershed.

Zach wouldn't have drunk beer. He wouldn't have taken off all his clothes and jumped naked into the Gulf (I'm getting to that part) the night Lourna and I suffered through his stupid bonfire-on-the-beach show of manhood. That night, while Zach danced around the fire, Lourna whispered in my ear, but I couldn't hear her over the wind.

Most of the guests in the beach condos behind us had switched off their lights. The cold wind drove away the mosquitos and whipped a stinging mist of sand off the dunes. The moon scuttled behind clouds and the stars began to flicker. I imagined Lourna in the condo cradling a glass of wine, crying under the lamp she pointed out when we first arrived, a lampshade covered in pink seashells. Her praise of the lamp was an obvious attempt to put a positive spin on a rental with mice poop on the kitchen floor and no HBO. Lourna would wait for me and her dumb husband to return from the beach. She'd bitch at *me* for staying with him.

I wiped the scene from my mind. Listen, Nelle, he'd sequestered us into this antediluvian (I'm shooting for *Webster's* second meaning of "antediluvian" since "ridiculously old-fashioned" suits him as well) male fantasy, but I blamed Lourna for not trying harder to keep him sober. Why would she give up so easily? Why not threaten to leave him?

—Can you put your shirt on, Dad? You're grossing me out.

Zach gave me a sad-ape frown, then returned to beating his chest.

Lourna folded her arms. —Sweetie, your dad's doing his thing. We can't stop him. There's nothing we can say to him. Boys will be boys. Let's go inside.

—Inside *where*? That crappy condo Dad rented with my college savings fund?

—Please don't be rude, Liz. We'll talk inside.

—Why?

My face had a way of scrunching up when I was angry. It was dark. I don't know if Lourna could see me. I probably looked ugly and menacing. We shouted. My hair dangled in my eyes. The empty beach and open waters and infinite starlight over our heads invited a level of sitcom histrionics we'd never have pulled off inside our stuffy house in Salterra, at least not without the neighbors calling the cops.

—I don't want to talk. I don't want to go inside.

—You'd rather stay here with your father? Look at him!

Zach waved his arms at the bonfire like it was a symphony he had to conduct.

—What's my choice? Watch him make a fool of himself, or listen to your little sob story about how your romantic getaway didn't pan out? Honestly, I'd rather stay here.

—Fine, have fun with your father.

Meanwhile Zach concerned himself with his dying symphony. He dug a trench with his hands, tossed in charred and still-flaming debris, and he poured on more propane. The flames leapt higher. He asked if I wanted to roast marshmallows. I said are you kidding me.

For a moment the wind died down and I could hear Zach say a few words to himself, then he started talking directly to me. —Swam the whole goddamn length of grandma's pool underwater when you were seven. Remarkable. We named you after her.

—Duh. You've told me a million times.

My legs were tired. I sat on a beach chair.

—You were a good swimmer before you became a know-it-all.

Zach plopped into a shallow pit of sand and crossed his legs like a Buddha. The fire flickered over his face and chest and gave him an otherworldly glow. I'd always assumed grownups got fat when they drank alcohol, but Lourna told me the opposite happened with Zach. He puffed out *after* he stopped drinking. So now would he get skinny if he kept drinking cans of cheap beer? —So, I said. Are you not gonna be a pastor anymore?

—Don't get your hopes up. He waved an ember out of his face. I watched the spark disappear over his right kneecap. His gut dipped over the waistband of his trunks and the sand caught in the dark hairs swirling around his belly button. —Minor setback.

—Not that I care, but are you and Mom getting a divorce?

Honestly, I didn't think we'd manage to exchange any words that night. With my limited knowledge of alcohol from drinking schnapps on top of Fred's studio, I'd assumed after twelve beers Zach would be slurring his words. I can't remember if he had any lunch. What he said next came out clear and unbroken, as if he'd been storing it up for a long time.

LIMITING FACTORS

"When living conditions in an area are good, a population will generally grow. Eventually environmental factors will cause the population to stop growing. A 'limiting factor' is an environmental factor that causes a population to decrease. Some limiting factors for populations are food, water, space, and weather conditions."

From a worksheet Elizabeth's social studies teacher gave me. That's right. Elizabeth called and asked to have her homework forwarded to Warm Springs so she doesn't slip too far behind in her classes. Told you she was smart. I'm so proud of her.

No, it doesn't bother me she telephoned Lourna and not her father. We share the same landline, so technically either one of us could have answered the phone call.

Where was I? Oh, yeah. Lester. The warehouse.

Cockroaches.

Inferno wasn't hauling in enough cash for Lester to stay afloat, so the Alejandro Brothers initially employed him for a few side jobs to gain his trust. Going out to somebody's apartment to make a delivery and collect cash. Small amounts at first. Less than ten grams. Or fifteen grams to Wyatt Hasselbach and his lady Kamila, a happy local couple expecting their first child.

That's how these things work. I'm speculating of course, but when I reunite with my daughter at the end of this story, when y'all gotta watch me listen to her for as long as *she* can stand it before she goes off to college and forgets her father, all my prophesies will come true.

Weather conditions.

South Padre has hurricanes. Salterra has droughts and floods. The pentecostals of my flock tend to use any number of extreme-weather events to remind folks about the Imminence of the Second Coming, but to be frank, Watershed isn't so hardcore. I respect those traditions, and we do want to move people with the Holy Spirit. We will never turn anyone away from Jesus. On the flipside, I'm not gonna sit here and preach End of Times.

Lester Hargreve and his hoodlums abducted me from my home shortly after we opened Watershed. When I heard them breaking the lock on the front door, I gave my wedding ring to Lourna. —This is about the church, I said. They don't want us here. It's intimidation. Lourna wanted to call the police, but I told her not to call anyone. I kissed Lourna on the mouth. —I love you, I said. I love Elizabeth. Go into her room and lock the door.

And I waited for my kidnappers. I sat on the edge of my bed. How did I know the break-in was related to the church? Men of God often find themselves persecuted. The Sanhedrin brought Jesus to Pilot to carry out the orders of crucifixion. The Bible says Pilot didn't want to kill Jesus. Pilot couldn't find much wrong with him. "What law did this man break?"

—What do y'all need? I asked the men. I'll cooperate.

The questions should have taken place in public, but Lester's men confronted me at home. I would consider them limiting factors. My wife and daughter already know I'm not a fraud. They know I'd die for my faith. Yes, I'd have preferred a public trial at Watershed Church in the middle of a sermon. If they'd shot me in cold blood like they did Bishop Romero in El Salvador, my congregants would've made me a martyr, and my death would further the Legacy of Christ Jesus. Folks, I'm not saying I wanna die yet, public or private. I've turned my life over to my Lord. He's the Decider. In any case, they didn't murder me.

The blindfold felt like a rough piece of burlap. They bound my arms and legs with duct tape and threw me into the trunk of somebody's car.

My body trembled. Now you know why I'd tremble later in the music room. A night I would reexperience on many other nights in the months ahead until Jesus set me free.

In the trunk of the car, I lay curled in the fetal position. The edge of a hard object, a crowbar, struck the bones of my spine. (No, I didn't crap in my pants, nor did I lie to Rachel in the music room. Crapping as a terrified kid doesn't always lead to crapping as a terrified adult.) Maybe some pee dribbled out my hose, like when you close the fly of your pajamas in the middle of the night, too sleepy to realize you haven't finished yet, but the cold wetness on my clothes came from glass jugs. All during the ride, glass jugs or bottles clinked together. Not all of them were corked. What spilled onto my face and feet smelled like cheap wine.

Some limiting factors needn't remain purely environmental. Say a town's bar serves only Mexican beer, or cheap wine like what I smelled on my body when Lester's men kidnapped me. Say you drink only rum. Or say the people moving in learned about the existence of kidnappers in your town. That might convince enough people to skip Salterra and look elsewhere. No matter how good the living conditions, a town cannot handle too many kidnappers.

In conclusion, when they took off the blindfold, I found myself duct-taped to an office chair inside a warehouse. I might go on to argue that if word got around about the existence of these kidnappers, say on live radio, Salterra residents would flee in droves, and despite its otherwise "good living conditions," kidnappers would cause the town's population to decline.

PLEASE TELL MY DAD I DON'T NEED HIS HELP

I've already told you, Nelle, this isn't a school paper. So Zach doesn't need to help me with my homework. Anyway, I finished the worksheet on limiting factors in like ten minutes, so easy. Now I'm reading *In the House of the Lord* by Robert Flynn. I have to do a book report.

It's good except the main character reminds me of my dad, so I might put it down and read something else. No offense, Mr. Flynn. Not that Pastor Zacharias would be capable of pulling a stunt like in your novel where the pilot crashes during the Great Crusade, not knowing the banner for JESUS he's pulling is too heavy for the plane.

Warm Springs. Such a drag.

Get it, *drag*? Sorry, Nelle. Not funny. You know what else is not funny?

Windows. Views of the freeway, cars racing by, the riverboats gliding along the river. "Splendid" views here in Warm Springs to punish the patient and prisoner. At night, I watch the tourists on the banks of the River Walk with their margaritas and rum punches.

I imagine death-smiles on their faces. Flies circle their plates. Enchiladas. Chips and queso. Burgers. Black flies.

We're all dying up here. Plenty of leftovers for the flies.

They give me a paper cone full of orange juice to swallow my pills, and I can barely swallow them. Not funny. The mirrors are not funny, either. Actually, I wouldn't call the sheet of metal bolted to the wall above the sink a mirror. More like my reflection smeared across the waxed fender of my dad's old Camaro. No glass allowed.

Not that I'd want to look at my face. My face isn't funny. The shower isn't funny. Doesn't have a door, so you'd wait for your roommate to leave for breakfast? Not that I'd shower, since water, holy or unholy, can kill you if enough toxins sink into your pores.

My roommate walking in on me naked and seeing the cuts on my legs. That wouldn't be funny. No hooks to hang a towel on, "towel" being their not-funny word for the thin abrasive rag you'd dry yourself with. What else, Nelle? The nurse who admitted me, in bright yellow scrubs with blue flowers and her stomach looking ready to burst. Her pregnancy didn't seem funny. Through her tight scrubs her belly unbuttoned while a second nurse checked the pockets of my jeans for drugs and sharp objects. Considering the main reason people end up at Warm Springs, I don't find the experience of sitting eye-level with a big womb holding Baby/Life funny. It's like they pick a pregnant nurse on purpose. They want to show you how wrong and pointless and pathetic your little attempt to check out of this world really was. Whatever importance you might have wanted to attach to the act, it doesn't matter. You're a number, a blip, a grain of sand.

There's always more Life on the Way.

The paper bag with the travel-size toothbrush, the bar of soap thin as Watershed's communion wafers, and the black comb. Okay, the black comb is funny. Considering how the teeth snapped off the first time I tried to comb my unwashed hair. Like the fork I used in the cafeteria when I tried to stab a syrup-drowned slice of canned peach. Plastic snaps before you can put it to good use. Forget cutting your skin with a plastic utensil.

Sharing one remote for an entire floor of TVs in every room? No metal handles or hooks in sight. That's not funny. The door to your room does not lock from the inside. How can anything be funny in a room meant to erase your identity?

Can you still be a human if you can't laugh or cry?

Sometimes I feel like I have no identity outside my letters to you, Nelle. Definitely not in the group therapy sessions, where the counselor wants you to answer the questions and fit in. You can't wear your pants after they've taken away your belt. You can't wear your shoes after they've taken away your shoelaces. You are a walking zombie. Pretty soon, after they mete out the pills you're to take every day, with orange juice, you will cease to exist.

Which *might* be funny, like, if you could see yourself vanishing from above.

HIM

I like how you're opening up, sweetheart, the part about your environment, but you haven't told Nelle what I told you on the beach. I'll let you say it, but let me say first: Don't you think a fellow WHO WAS KIDNAPPED deserves to put back a few beers?

HER

No, because I don't believe you were kidnapped. I think you made up the story to have something to tell the congregation. A ridiculous excuse to become a Lost Drinking Fellow who got Saved. Only problem is you're not a "fellow." You're a pastor. No, I don't think a person in your situation deserves to "put back a few beers." Plus, they weren't a "few." They were twelve. Plus, you're not a "kid." You're an adult. So find another word for "kidnapped."

Also, I thought you were my dad.

Who made *my dad* disappear? That's what I'm wondering.

WALK IN ALL OF HIS WAYS

We're not always a snake with two heads slithering in opposite directions. We're a two-part invention. We have our own melodic lines or parts, but my part's been around longer than hers, so every now and then she must listen to me. Nothing in the world Elizabeth hates more than hearing me give directions.

And yet the Bible says follow the Way. You gotta fear the Lord. You gotta love the Lord. You gotta serve Him with *all* your heart and soul. Walk in *all* of his ways.

In the warehouse, a roach scurried over my left foot, rubbed my toe with its antennae, and froze, as if it wanted to crawl up my pants. I smashed it with my bare heel, but only caught the head, and the body scattered off leaving a wake of its milk-colored blood and guts.

Y'all know a roach can live for more than seven days without its head? Apparently they can breathe through holes all over their body, so if they lose the head they don't suffocate. It takes about a week before they die of dehydration. Flies crawled along my arms. One landed on my upper lip. Roaches haven't found a way to drink from other parts of their body.

Compared to the bugs and the waiting, Lester Hargreve's entrance sort of came as a relief. He barged in through a side door with an AK-47. I assumed it was an AK-47. It had the wooden stock and handguard, gas piston above the receiver, and curved magazine.

Like I say at our men's Bible Study, a pastor shouldn't know so much about guns.

Under the bay lights that hung from chains in a stratosphere of pink glass wool and air ducts, Lester sported a Rebel flag do-rag soiled with motor grease, a hermit's gray beard, gold hoop earrings, and a plaid shirt with sleeves rolled to expose skin tattooed with a skull-and-bones, sharks' teeth, baby seahorses, and a giant squid. There were more tattoos, but the machine gun with the curved magazine, what the Mexicans call a *cuerno de chivo*, "a goat horn," capable of firing thirty rounds of lethal 39mm cartridges with a muzzle velocity of over two thousand feet per second—that baby demanded more of my attention.

—Pastor, you're shaking like a reed. You need a blanket?

—No. What do you want from me?

My teeth did chatter. A ganglion cyst, round and slightly reddened like a gumball, protruded from the back of Lester's left hand. When Lester's finger slid into the trigger hold, the cyst appeared to wobble. His paint-splattered blue jeans had grass stains and holes in the kneecaps and the cuffs were tucked into a pair of gray rubber boots.

—Got your own church now? He shook his head. —I don't fucking believe it.

—Heard the gospel of Christ? Come join us.

Lester slung the AK-47 over his shoulder. He pulled a chair up in front of me and sat on it backwards, his inked arms folded over the back rest. The cyst bulged like it wanted me to stick a needle in it and see what oozed out. I almost vomited in my mouth. Lester took obvious pleasure in watching me sit with my arms duct-taped to the chair, nauseated and scared.

—I would like to offer you a business opportunity.

I thought, Watershed would like to offer you Salvation, but I probably only asked if he'd like to have a more civil meet-and-greet at my church.

—Glad we can speak freely, old friend. Lester thumbed a drumroll on the back of the chair. —I'm not asking you to drink at my bar. Why'd you think I'd want to sing songs at your church? I'm talking about a chance to make a lot of money. Easy-peasy.

—"Don't store up for yourselves treasures on earth," the Bible says, "where moth and rust consume and where thieves break in and steal. Store up for yourselves treasures in heaven, where neither moth nor rust consumes and where thieves do not break in and steal. For where your treasure is, there your heart will be also."

—We're in a warehouse. I take a look around here. I don't see any treasures. I see emptiness. I didn't see treasures when I lived by the ocean, either. The tourists would talk of paradise, but no buried treasure. Only sad old men with their metal detectors, waving their sad broken wands up and down the beach all morning.

—You loved the ocean, Lester. I remembered that about you.

—Not from where I was standing. Now I know how to love it. There's no such thing as buried treasure. You can't search for wealth. You have to create it. Those sad old men, you know what they looked like? Prisoners. Prisoners walking up and down a prison yard. Up and down all morning. Only they didn't realize they were chained. I was chained. I'm going to free myself.

—You're mistaken. I'll pray for you.

—You want to grow your church? You want to make disciples out of them? We were brothers who couldn't fish, remember? Work with me. We'll be fishers of men.

—You're trying to speak my language so I'll work with you. We're not the same, Lester. I've found Jesus. I don't care about money. I might be shaking like a reed, but I hear the fear and trembling in your voice. You've gotten tangled up with some bad actors, haven't you? I don't know what you did, but only Jesus can save you now.

Lester didn't care about my church. He needed money. A brother who couldn't fish? We were never brothers. He was tired of taking crumbs. He had bigger dreams. Lester wanted to cast a net wide enough to return to South Padre on his own terms. He'd buy the Bait & Wait. He'd buy the whole island, as many properties as he could, build an empire.

Lester understood an important truth about business: you either own the system or the system owns you. Right now the Alejandro Brothers owned him. They'd gotten to him. They would use him. For him to slip out of their grip and free himself, he'd have to use me.

—God's will, I said, I'll grow my church by preaching the truth.

—Trust me. God wants you to take this opportunity.

—What if I choose not to work with you, Lester?

From inside his boot Lester pulled out a fillet knife with fish scales on the blade. He pressed the tip of the knife into his unkempt beard and twirled it in circles. The blade, the smell, the tumor. All of it clunked down my stomach.

—Wonder why those men didn't go after your family?

A buzzing sound. I blew sharply out of my nostrils. The fly landed at my feet on the cement, resurrected itself, and followed the roach-gut path under Lester's chair.

STARE LONG ENOUGH AT THE SEA

And the sea will stare back you. That's what Zach said, or what I think he said. He stood with his back to me and the bonfire. —It's cold, Dad. Time to head in.

—Lazarus was dead four days before Jesus brought him back to life. How cold you think he was? You imagine what he smelled like?

—Gross. I'd rather not.

—Praise Him, Elizabeth. Can you at least praise Him once, and recognize the miracle He works in all of us? God hates moaning. He hears everything. How about we make a deal? I'll tell you one honest thing I've never told anybody before, and you tell me one honest thing.

—Something I haven't told anyone before?

Zach turned. Wild firelight danced in his eyes. —Not even Mom. But it's got to be truthful, honest, a real thing. Lies and inventions don't count in this game.

—Fine, I said. Your idea, you go first.

Zach closed his eyes, opened them. —I got lost the day you were born.

—I bet you did. Nobody gave you directions to the hospital.

—Sweetheart, that's not what I mean. I got *lost*. I was a man. I was a husband. When you were born, they told me I was a father. My father left us too soon.

—So now you're jumping ship as well. How convenient.

—I'm not jumping ship. I'm not leaving. I'm trying to get you to see something, Elizabeth. I want you to understand I didn't know how to be a good father. It's not written in a manual they hand out at the hospital. It's not encoded in the bylaws of Methodist Healthcare Ministries. I had nobody to model myself after. I needed a better guide.

Down the beach from us, a giant octopus hovered inches above the sand, with luminous eyeballs fixed to each of its eight legs. The eyeballs bounced around in the darkness, independent of one another. The screams of young kids alerted us to what was really going on: fiddler-crab spear hunting. The kids, mostly boys, each had taped a flashlight and kitchen knife to the end of a broom handle, and they were all running around in the swirling sand, stabbing fiddler crabs as they emerged from their finger-width tunnels to crawl out into the light.

—All right, I said to Zach. I sort of understand, but why can't we do normal family stuff? (I watched the kids race over the dunes.) Why is it always so spiritual and serious?

—And now I see what you're going through, he said, the demons you're wrestling with, and I'm sorry. I just want to tell you it's my fault. I should've been a better father.

—Hey, Zach. News flash. I'm not wrestling any demons! I'm fine.

But I wasn't fine. I knew this. His words had clawed at me and reached in and pulled at something, a sadness I'd kept hidden beneath all my sarcasm, frustration, and anger. I clutched the towel around my shoulders, trying to keep warm, but the wind blew through it and gave me goosebumps. I dug my toes in the sand. The cold inched up through my legs.

—You're not fine. If it's your one honest thing, so be it. I want to help.

I couldn't believe I was still on the beach, Nelle. I didn't trust Zach, but I was making an honest effort to see things from his point of view. Maybe his leaving Salterra was a form of rebellion. He'd gotten fed up with his duties. He finally realized the responsibility was preventing him from connecting with his daughter. But that's like a big "maybe," which we'd have to put in bold font, all caps. **MAYBE**. Maybe he needed this escape from being a Man of God long enough to see me for who I was—not religious, not remotely religious, only a dutiful sad frightened girl whose life had been uprooted over one man's Calling from God.

—Okay, I said, but if I'm not fine, you're not fine, either. Ever since Fred Valenkemp arrived, you've been acting weird. The night you disappeared, you went on a bender.

—Is that what your mother told you?

—She didn't tell me. I just assumed. What you're doing now confirms my assumption. You went out and got drunk and felt guilty. You came back all strange, you took an hour-long shower, and you didn't talk to either of us. (I had no idea about the Alejandro Brothers, Nelle, nor did I know what Lester had done to him, and if Zach had told me that night, I wouldn't have believed him. So I was going with the bender theory.) —Just admit it, Zach.

—No, I didn't. The honest thing was, well, I can't tell you. Not about that night. Not yet. All I can say is I strayed from the Path, like I've done all my life. The forces of evil, those demonic forces of moral turpitude, I didn't have the strength to refuse, so I submitted. I asked my Father for help, but he wasn't speaking to me that night. He wasn't telling me what to do.

—Nobody's telling me what to do, either. I'm only thirteen, but you don't see me heading off to South Padre with a cooler of beer. Getting drunk and dancing around a bonfire.

—You don't face the same pressures I do.

—You mean I don't have as many "life experiences"? So what. I'm old enough to see what the church has done to our family. It's ruining us.

Up until that night, Nelle, I'd maintained some level of detachment, fooling myself into thinking I didn't care enough to try to talk him into abandoning Watershed. Fooling myself into thinking I could leave this crazy family any time I wanted, because I didn't care, but now I was starting to feel sorry for him. I was starting to actually care. He'd reached his claws in and tugged, and maybe I'd let him tug and hold too long.

He looked up at me and at the night sky. —You're probably right. I should give up the church, but I can't. There are lives at stake.

—You mean souls? Can't these people go somewhere else?

—No, I mean *lives*. Yours, mine, your mother's. I'm scared.

I'd never heard him like this before. Usually people confessed their fears to *him*. Usually he was the fearless one. He must have sensed we were at an impasse: I couldn't help him, and I wouldn't let him help me. He got up and brushed the sand from his legs. He stumbled towards the ocean and picked up what looked like a chunk of stale bread.

—The body of Christ? Now if we only had some wine.

—Wait, Zach. Where are you going? Listen, I'm scared, too. Don't leave.

(Nelle, if you become a parent one day and your teenage daughter sits stone-faced in the passenger seat after you pick her up from school and starts burning a plastic bag with the car's cigarette lighter, out of boredom, and you freak because you think your daughter "has gone pyro," or whatever—if this happens, if she's silent when you ask her why, or if she replies in such a way that you're convinced she doesn't care if she burns her fingers, herself, you, your car, the rest of your family—Nelle-of-the-Future, it's not like she has more important things on her mind, so keep asking questions even if you think it's pointless. Show interest in her when she doesn't show interest in anything except burning a plastic bag in the car and watching the paper inside turn to golden embers. So she knows. [It's not weird to ask questions.])

Zach continued down the beach. I followed him. He held onto the bread with one hand and carved אֲדֹנָי* in the sand with a branch of driftwood. Somewhere between the water and me he took a bite of the bread and rolled the grit around on his tongue. He didn't spit it out. I guess one bite was enough. He tossed the bread and driftwood into the sea.

—Lord, he shouted. Defend me against the armies of Satan!

He slid off his trunks and ran naked into the water. The crack in his moon bobbed up and down while his front parts combatted the chilly waves.

Okay, I said to myself. One honest, real thing. If my family's weird, *we're all freaking weird*. Now where in the hell is he going?

---

* 'adonai / my Lord / my Master (divine title)

SAMSON AND DUH-LYING WON'T GET YOU INTO HEAVEN

Tonight I want to talk to you about Samson, a man whose birth was a miracle in every way. Forget what you heard about Samson back in Sunday school. Forget about the girl who came along and cut Samson's beautiful hair and robbed him of his strength. There is so much more to the story. Yes, Samson was the last Judge of Israel. Yes, he slayed a lion with his bare hands. Yes, he defeated a whole army of Philistines with the jawbone of a donkey.

Did you know Samson wasn't supposed to be born?

That's right. Samson's mother was not supposed to have any children. She was old and barren, and she and her husband Manoah had all but given up the idea of having kids.

The Lord does amazing things, folks. Where there is nothing, the Lord creates something. Where there is hopelessness, the Lord creates Hope.

Normally in this part of the service, I'd breathe into the microphone, let you know how hard I'm working to deliver the Lord's Promise. I'd pause for dramatic effect. I'd stare out at the audience and nod, almost like I'm challenging you to say I'm wrong about the Lord's Promise. Am I wrong about the Lord's Promise? An Angel of the Lord visited Samson's mother and told her she'd have a child. Can you believe it? Her husband didn't believe it. Manoah said you're too old, woman. But Samson's mother believed. Her faith was like a pit bull, folks. Once she latched on, the jaws of her pit-bull faith would never let go.

Never mess with a momma with a pit bull, ladies and gentlemen.

We serve a God who makes the impossible possible. Can I get an amen? We serve a God who makes the unseen *seen*. We serve a God who makes the unfathomable a reality. We serve a God who can take nothing and make it into something. Romans 4 says, "He calls things into being that are not." That's the kind of God we serve.

Samson's mother latched on to her faith like a pit bull, and she would not let go. Mothers, I want you all to latch on, all right? Latch on and keep praying, and God is gonna see a way through. God is not gonna fail you. He hears everything.

Fred heard everything, too.

—I know what's been going on at night, Fred told me. I've heard them.

We were having a barbecue at the Valenkemps when Fred said this. What's more American than a barbecue? One minute I'm watching him squeeze lighter fluid onto a mound of charcoal, the next minute he's whispering to me about how he could hear the Alejandro Brothers and their thugs at night, working to hide their product in my church.

—Well, I said, stunned. I'm not sure I know what you're talking about.

—Oh, I think you do.

I took out a piece of gum, popped it in my mouth, and chewed. Smoke from the charcoal drifted up and watered my eyes. The peppermint gum failed to lubricate the wad of cotton forming inside my mouth. Fred said he had to remove his equipment from the music room.

—I can't risk destruction, he said. People always mess with your stuff.

—Whatever you may have seen or overheard, I have nothing to do with it, I promise.

—They come and go at night. They move with efficiency, and they always clean up after themselves. I like a clean workspace. Still, I can't keep my equipment in there.

—Fred, I'm sorry. Listen, it's important we don't interfere.

—They must have gotten to you. Fred spoke in a blunt tone. He squinted and nodded. Yes, I believe they got to you.

He turned back to the grill and threw on the steaks.

—It's got nothing to do with me, Fred. I swear. They're only here for a short time. You don't have to worry about your equipment. I promise, they're not interested in taking your stuff. As long as we don't bother them, they'll do their thing and leave us alone. You're important to us, my Brother. To everyone. I'll do whatever it takes to keep you with us at Watershed.

—Who said I was leaving?

The charcoal hissed as the marble fat slid off the steaks, dripped through the bars of the grill, and sizzled over the ashes. I rubbed my eyes, glanced at the back door, praying our wives would stay inside. If I couldn't explain to Lourna what we were still doing here in Salterra, how would I be able to explain it to Rachel and the girls?

—I'm glad you're not leaving, Fred. I'm not leaving. None of us are.

Fred flipped the steaks with a pair of metal tongs. After searing the meat for a couple of minutes, he dragged the steaks to the far side of the grill. —Better let these cool off.

I should tell y'all, Fred didn't have any normal Weber charcoal grill. He'd dug a four-foot hole in his yard, filled it with pea gravel, and lined the hole with cinder blocks. His fire pit had a giant grill the size of a rig's hubcap. Between Fred's smoking fire pit and the neighbors burning all their dead brush, it's a wonder nobody called the fire department.

After he pulled the steaks off the grill and wrapped them in foil, we gathered in the kitchen, and I said a prayer for God to bless this glorious union of our two families.

My daughter had been hanging out with Nelle in her room. They had a funny smell on them, like peach cobbler sitting out to long, fermented, but never mind. They were happy. I was happy. While we let the meat sweat it out, Rachel showed us around the house. Fred had installed an automatic lighting system that allowed you to lower or raise the brightness of your ceiling lights by whistling a downward or upward glissando.

—We should get one for our house, I said, forgetting Lourna couldn't whistle.

Liz said something inaudible, giggled, and hiccupped.

—I'm so glad y'all decided to buy the Robertsons' house, I said. We were wondering if anybody would buy this old place. We love what you've done with it.

—We haven't done much, Rachel said. Still trying to make time.

In truth, I didn't notice anything new about the house. I didn't notice their furniture, the rugs, the tables, the dressers, the pictures on the wall. I didn't notice anything until Rachel took me back weeks later, the night of our Thursday rehearsal, when we were looking for Fred. All I could think about now was how much Fred had seen or heard, whether he was sincere when he said he'd stay in Salterra. The church needed him. My Praise Team needed him. His ivory tickling brought us all together. No church in South Texas employed a better keyboardist. His contemporary sound, his pedal effects, his electrifying chords—but more than his music, let's call it his presence. Yes, his quiet stable presence raised us out of the swale we'd been living in. New Foundations never had a Fred Valenkemp. After my brother died, I prayed for his return. I cried aloud to the Lord, and when Fred showed up that morning at Watershed with his suitcases, when Fred worked his magic, I said to myself, Something has changed. This one's different. I cried to the Lord, and He answered me from His holy mountain.

—We like it here, Fred told us. It's a crazy world. Nice to be in one place.

—I know what you mean, Brother. I know what you mean.

Like Samson, Fred wasn't supposed to be born, folks. Fred's mother was forty-three when she had him, Rachel told me. His mother went to the hospital for a procedure, and the doctor broke the news. The doctor said, You're going to have a baby. Fred's mother didn't believe him. The doctor said, In fact, you have conceived a child. Like Samson, Fred came into this world in a miraculous way. An only child, Fred was lonely and shy. He had not found his calling. (He had not found his vital role as a member of our Praise Team.) So naturally he got into trouble. After school he'd go knocking on doors to ask if any kids could hang out with him. The neighborhood kids found him strange. Fred mistook their curiosity for friendship.

He'd do anything for attention, Rachel said. During an assembly at his elementary school one time, Fred dropped a cherry bomb in the toilet of the boys room, to get everybody to flee the auditorium. Once he convinced a neighborhood kid to loan him a toy soldier, Rachel said. We're talking about one of those green-plastic Army guys, with a machine gun molded to the arms, a puddle-shaped platform attached to the boots to keep the soldier upright.

Fred grabbed the soldier and held it over the stove. He clicked on the pilot light. Dipped the soldier in blue flame. The noises Fred made to imitate the sound of a burning man, Rachel told me, made the hairs on the back of her neck stand. The flame melted off the arms, legs, and head, leaving a black stump. Little Fred showed his friend how to burn popcorn in the microwave to mask the stench of charred plastic.

There's a parallel with Samson's father, folks. If you'll bear with me. Manoah made an offering to the Angel of the Lord, thanking him for his miracle son. The Angel told Manoah not to give thanks to him but to God. The Angel of the Lord touched the offering with his staff and it burst into flames, and the Angel rode the flames on back to heaven.

—I'm not leaving any time soon, Fred told me while we were cutting into the steaks. When I do leave, though, I'd like to go out like Samson.

—Go out? What do you mean *go out*?

—I figure I have two or three more concertos in me. Three at most.

—I didn't realize you still composed, Fred. That's wonderful.

—It is, wonderful. He glanced at his fingers, stained with purple ink. He'd been composing all morning. Later I'd find out he wrote with a fountain pen on staff paper. He used a type of ink called Shaeffer. It smelled like grapes.

—Two or three more concertos, he said, then I'm ready to leave. And I'd like to go out with a brutal collision of sound. All the people who doubted me? Who didn't believe I could write music? All the naysayers? They'd stick around and listen, and they'd be so enraptured, they'd never want the music to end. I'd take them out with me.

The whole table went silent for a moment.

—Fred, you don't get to decide how you die. That's up to God.

He nodded, but I don't think he was listening to me. He'd trotted off into his own magical realm of eighth notes and polyphonic structures and Romantic suicides.

I thought of my brother, bleeding from his head after hitting a bad stretch of ice in Arizona. —God decides when it's your time. Not you.

—Samson decided. He pulled down the temple of Dagon, did he not?

—Fred, these steaks are delicious. Thank y'all for having us over.

Praise Him this evening, folks. His promise is coming. He's going to make a way where there used to be no way. He's going to make it greater than you could ever imagine. This is the kind of God we serve. Ephesians 3:20 says, "Now to him who is able to do immeasurably more than all we can ask or imagine, according to his power that is at work within us."

That's the kind of God we serve.

Awesome. Samson is a miracle.

—Did he not pull down the temple of Dagon to destroy his enemies?

Normally in this part of the service I'd have everyone stand together and read our scripture aloud. Judges 13:3, y'all. Can we read this passage together?

The Angel of the Lord appeared to Manoah's wife and said, "Even though you have been unable to have children, you will soon become pregnant and give birth to a son. So be careful; you must not drink wine or any other alcoholic drink nor eat any forbidden food. You will become pregnant and give birth to a son, and his hair must never be cut. For he will be dedicated to God as a Nazirite from birth. He will begin to rescue Israel from the Philistines."

Father, we thank you for your word this evening. I just pray Father, my King, that you anoint me to preach your Word. Fred's words went in my ear and out the other because he was not God's anointed. It's a shame how he died, but at least he wasn't able to *take them out.*

At least God foiled his evil plans.

Father, it's your Word that's sharper than any two-edged sword. Your Word, that cuts the bone from the marrow. Cuts the fat off the best T-bone steak I'd ever eaten in my life. (Fred knew how to grill.) Your Word, Lord, that changes us from the inside out. Your Word, that penetrates our hearts. That tears right through all the layers of fat we cloak around our hearts when we live in darkness. We pray, Father God, it will be You speaking through us. It will be all of You and none of us. In Jesus' name. Amen.

Yes, God was raising up somebody named Samson. God was raising up a miracle boy. Samson was chosen before he was born, just like you. He was known in his mother's womb, like you. He was set apart and called to be holy and righteous, just like you. He was a miracle that caused people to say only God could have done that, in that boy's life, just like you.

Before Samson was born, Manoah said to his wife, "I want to hear from the Angel of the Lord myself. Will you ask him to come?" Manoah prayed for the Angel to appear, and the Angel did appear once again but not to Manoah. He appeared to Manoah's wife. She stood in the middle of the field and called to her husband, "Manoah, come quick! He's here." And there Manoah saw the Angel. He looked at him and asked him. In Judges 13:17, Manoah asks the Angel of the Lord, "What's your name? Because if what you have said happens, we'll glorify you." And the Angel of the Lord answers him, "Why are you asking about my name? It's Wonderful." It's wonderful. This is awesome. Simply awesome. Isaiah 9:6 says, "For unto us a child is born, to us a Son is given, and the government will be on his shoulders. And He will be called *Wonderful* Counselor, Mighty God, Everlasting Father, Prince of Peace." Amen.

CROOKED RAIN, CROOKED RAIN

It wasn't wonderful what we did to Fred Valenkemp, but I do believe it was necessary. Okay, maybe we had too much schnapps before the barbecue. Maybe my giggling gave us away, but I didn't think Fred's steaks were all that great. Sal's BBQ serves better brisket. That's a fact.

Where was Zach when Fred was running his mouth about wanting to take everybody out in his Temple of Watershed? Why didn't Zach intervene? Get Fred to shift gears?

Zach couldn't get out from behind his brother's Willie G. Special. That's why. The brother who shall remain nameless presented a massive blind spot to Fred's psychopathic tendencies. It's snowing in Arizona. Yeah, well, it's snowing in Florida.

It's snowing in Texas.

That's what we'd say to a girl who wears a shirt that doesn't cover up her bra. Whatever her name starts with, you pick a state of the same letter. So if it's Terresa whose undergarments are on display in class, we'd shout: It's snowing in Texas!

If it's Fiona, It's snowing in Florida! You get the idea.

Also, it's snowing in Oregon if Mr. Owen in Pre-Algebra has dandruff on his sweater. Which is always. Except we don't say it to his face because he'll give us detention.

At Warm Springs all the male nurses have dandruff. And some of the females. With my music privileges restored, I'm listening to the new Pavement, *Crooked Rain, Crooked Rain*. Pretty cool album. I turn up the volume all the way, and I respect how Steven Malkmus admits he doesn't know what the hell Smashing Pumpkins is singing about. Nobody does.

Even Billy Corgan doesn't know what Smashing Pumpkins is singing about. It's like in that dream where you're chasing a lion, and the lion turns around and says, Stop chasing me, and you didn't know the lion could talk. A talking lion. You don't know what it means.

Just like nobody knows what Fred meant when he said he had two or three more concertos in him. Concertos? Yeah, right. Was that really what he'd played for us when he auditioned in the barn? I wouldn't have called it a concerto. It sounded too improvised, too chaotic. It wasn't even coherent. And he didn't have any more songs in his studio. At least, not anything written down. We searched the place, Nelle. We tore his studio apart. Found nothing except a few scratches of ink on a sheet of yellow paper that looked like it'd sat in his drawer for decades. Nothing you'd call a composition, much less a concerto.

We should've told Zach the barbecue and the house and that bit about "staying in one place" were all lies. Fred would've lied his way to heaven if he could get away with it. He never intended to settle down. He wasn't like Zach, who had the church to keep him tethered to Salterra. Fred wouldn't stay in one place. He'd drag his family behind him for the rest of his life.

We should've told Zach he's never going to understand Fred Valenkemp. Listen to Malkmus. Not Manoah. There's nothing wrong with admitting what you can't understand.

IN THE RECOVERY ROOM

A few words about Elizabeth's birth before I motor y'all back to the warehouse with me in the chair and Lester with his AK-47 trained on my forehead: Lourna sailed past her due date by a week or two, as did both her sisters before her, so we weren't alarmed when her obstetrician recommended she come to the hospital early to induce labor. It was a Wednesday. Not much doing in the studio, so I drove Lourna to Methodist where we checked her into a nice private room, and the doctors welcomed her and administered a hormone called oxytocin.

From the Greek, Liz. *Oxus tokos.* Sharp child-birth.

—Your baby's going to be fine, the nurse said. This will give her a little nudge.

"A little nudge." Funny.

After an anxious RN stabbed Lourna's wrist twice with the needle for the IV, and failed twice to find a vein, blood pouring like Christ's wounds on the cross, the clear IV tube pumped the oxytocin into her bloodstream, and I'd say within half an hour the "little nudge" had turned into lacerating waves of pain. Her body shut down. Her face tightened. She balled her hands into fists. She drew inward. Like a sick animal hiding itself to stay safe from predators.

The sweat broke across her forehead and beaded on the parts of her skull visible beneath her hair someone had tightened into a ponytail.

Lourna sat up, bent at the waist, shut her eyes, and squeezed my hand. She didn't look at me. She didn't respond to my asking her if she was all right, so I stopped asking. The pressure of her fingers around my hand intensified. My hand got real sore. I didn't dare move.

Not to compare my wife to an animal, but she seemed to have this instinct to withdraw from human contact, as if she understood communicating would not restore her to life. I wished somebody could've reminded me she wasn't dying. She was having a baby.

I wouldn't know what dying looked like until years later when I became a pastor, when I'd visit my parishioners, many of whom were days if not hours from actually dying. I'd learn a lot from them. Dying humans don't hide. The dying ask questions. They want to know where they're going, when they'll get there, what it was like for the friends or family who went before them. Until the morphine hits, they hold your hand and look you in the eye and hold your attention, as if conversing could stave off the final end.

The weak and injured hide. The dying come into view. They might be silent at times, but I do believe the dying are eager to engage with us while they still can.

Hours went by. Eight, ten, twelve. My wife crunched into a ball of pain. I told the nurse I didn't think the oxy-whatever was working. Everything was taking too long. —Go, take a break, Lourna said.

—You sure? I said. —Yeah, fine. —Okay, I'll go to the cafeteria. You want anything? —No. —You sure? Some water? —Stop asking questions. *Go.*

I went downstairs and stood in the cafeteria line.

Before I could pay for my coffee, my brother ran over and asked me if I'd heard.

—Heard what? What's wrong?

—The doctor said to put these on. My brother threw me a folded pair of green scrubs wrapped in clear plastic. —He said put these on and hurry back upstairs.

I dropped my change, left the coffee, and charged upstairs with the scrubs held to my chest like it was the nuclear football and I had to decide how this would all end. I tore the pants yanking them over my loafers.

By the way, when Elizabeth tells you I would make stupid toasts on the beach to "some uncle she never met," she's talking about the brother who ran down to find me in the cafeteria, the guy who threw me the scrubs and told me to get upstairs where they were about to perform an emergency cesarean on Lourna after the monitor showed a stress-induced arrhythmia in the baby. Not even born yet, and my daughter's heart was already stressed out. Same brother who stood with me while the doctors rolled Lourna into surgery and put the paper shower cap on her head and a paper curtain around her belly.

Same brother who stood with me behind a small window of fire-proof glass on the other side of which my wife lay on a bed with cords taped to her skin and an oxygen mask like the one I wore when our church burned to the ground. Same brother who heard the nurse tell us we couldn't stand there, so she led us into a recovery room, where we listened to the din of sweaty women moaning in varying states of semi-consciousness as their anesthesia wore off.

You met him, Elizabeth. The day you were born. Unfortunately he didn't live to see you grow up. But he held you in the hospital. I remember. My brother looked into your eyes, touched your gummy cheeks. He counted your ten perfect fingers, your ten perfect toes.

THE DUNGEON AND "DOUBLE DRAGON"

Hard for a murderer to write about her victim without sounding biased. Even if I showed Fred in his own words, you wouldn't understand why he needed to go. All daughters betray their fathers by growing up. Not every daughter needs to betray her father when she's young, but we had to do more than pour Palmolive into Fred's peach schnapps. Put more than liquid Tide in his coffee. Fun shenanigans aren't the same as real crimes. We should've used antifreeze.

Honestly, what kind of man drinks peach schnapps? He probably left it in his liquor cabinet for *us* to drink. I never heard him enter the studio. Fred's door didn't whine like at our house. I'm guessing he filled the door and walls of his studio with mineral wool. He snuck in behind me and sailed past his desk, but not without saying a few words.

—Is that supposed to be for me?

The brown clay mug had a sideways crooked-smile handle, as if pinched into place by the fingers of a child. Maybe you made it for him in art class years ago, Nelle. The dribbles of detergent next to the mug were Caribbean blue. I'd had some trouble opening the heavy jug of Tide. So shoot me. I'd meant to wipe up the spill, hide the paper towels. I ran out of time.

—Nelle dared me, I said.

—Nelle's not here, he said.

—No, I said. She's in the house. I told her it wouldn't work.

—You always lie to adults?

—It's true. I told her you'd smell the Tide before you took a sip. Or you'd take a sip and spit out the soap. I touched the crooked handle and turned the mug in a circle.

—You should put some soap on those cuts. And run cold water.

—What? I felt my face turn red.

Fred pulled what I thought was a black handkerchief out of his pocket (it was a piece of synthetic microfiber used to clean musical instruments). I thought he was going to wipe my thigh or something, but he went to his rack of synthesizers and rubbed the cloth over the keys of a Roland Juno-60. He turned on the synthesizer and played it with a patch he called a "space harp." I didn't get it. The "harp" part, I mean. The notes sounded all tinny and alien, like the background music for Double Dragon. You know, the arcade game? Where in the intro the dude in the hot-pink muscle shirt punches the woman in the stomach?

—That's not "outer space," I said, my face burning. My cat scratched me.

—You don't have a cat. I'm right. You always lie to adults.

He played the video-game music again. The words "Insert Coin" flashed before me in a fuzzy yellow font. On screen, the muscle-shirt dude punched the girl in the stomach and flipped her onto his shoulder. When he hauled her away with his gang, everyone could see her panties.

I uncuffed my dungaree shorts to cover more of my thighs.

But Fred had seen my wounds.

Nobody except my parents had seen them. After that one time in the car on the way back from South Padre. Nelle, why didn't you tell me Fred was coming home early? His "soap and run cold water" sounded smart-alecky. He only cared about his stupid gadgets. When he finished the outer-space theme, Fred swiveled in his chair, rubbed his feet over the carpet.

—Run cold water over the cuts and use a bar of soap, not liquid detergent.

—Thanks for the tip. I thought you were in New York.

He grabbed the black cloth and rubbed it gently across a few cables that stuck out under a speaker or subwoofer mounted four or five feet above the ground, almost the same height as his vertical keyboard rack. —You and Nelle do whatever you want at my desk, but this side of the studio? He gestured toward his synthesizers, the suitcases open on the floor, the boxy computer and keyboard on the card table, big silver studio headphones, and a mixing board with hundreds of colored knobs, buttons, and volume sliders. —This side of my studio? This is where I keep my equipment. You do not go near my equipment. Understood?

—Whatever. No problem. Why don't you lock your door, man?

—You don't touch anything. You don't plug in anything. You don't think about plugging in anything. You don't put water anywhere except on those cuts before they become infected. All this gear is expensive. And it's *real*. Not like your father's piano. I do keep the door locked, but Nelle must have found the key. Or you found it. Either way, you're busted.

—Okay, what do you mean not like my father's piano?

—The Baldwin Hamilton. At Freedom Keys. It's hollow.

—What's that mean? Out of tune?

—There's nothing inside. No strings. No soundboard.

Surrounded by his gear, he squinted and spoke in a snotty tone I don't think he would've used at Watershed. Definitely not around the other adults. Clearly, I was in his "dungeon," so he could treat me how he wanted. He could talk to me however he wanted. I was the one in trouble, so he wasn't afraid I'd tell my dad about our conversation. And if I did, it wouldn't matter. Fred knew my dad needed him more than he needed my dad. Fred could lecture me, he could threaten me, he could treat me like the girl in Double Dragon. Here he was the muscle-shirt dude.

—I've been watching your dad, he said.

—Why?

I went to the door but I didn't leave. Walking out would've been a gift to him. A swift exit to magnify my shame after having been caught putting Tide in his coffee. Plus, the cutting. He understood something about me. A person who can look at you in an instant and act and sound like they already *know* you—that's a dangerous person.

—Your father do that to you? he said.

—Maybe, I said. Standing up, I know Fred couldn't see my cuts anymore, yet I kept pulling on the hem of my dungarees, as if to unroll the cuffs. —Maybe not.

—If he did, it's child abuse. I'll have to report it.

He slid his hands along his thighs and he stared at my thighs.

—It's required by law, he said. (He never reported it, Nelle. So what's that tell you about him? Witnessing lacerations on a girl, on a minor? Asking her about them, hearing her say "maybe, maybe not," and then *not* telling the cops? I'd say that's neglect. Worse than lying about a stupid prank. I'd say it's letting child abuse *happen*.)

—Why are you watching my dad?

—He talks to a lot of people.

—Of course he talks to a lot of people. He's a pastor.

—Did you see him talking to the sheriff?

—No.

—Well, he did.

—Go ahead, report him. I don't care.

—Why do you think your dad keeps an empty piano?

—I don't know. He's dumb?

—After he talked to the sheriff, he talked to my wife, Nelle's mom.

—Yeah, I know Nelle's mom is your wife, Fred.

He rubbed his hands along his thighs and then together like when you're cold and you've made a campfire. He flashed me his straight white teeth—I guess you could call it a smile—then his mouth collapsed into a blank expression.

—Rachel's nice. People sometimes take advantage. Of her being so nice. I don't like my wife talking to your dad. Don't like how it looks.

—Are you still going to report my dad? That'd be *nice* if you did. You should report him *and* my mom. Now I'm gonna skedaddle.

—All I'm saying is, your dad better not talk to my wife again.

—Are you threatening us? I could tell him, you know.

—Your dad won't believe you. He thinks I'm his best friend. He thinks he knows me.

The pauses in his speech would've scared me if I didn't think he was so weird.

—They say y'all are Christians. I don't care. If your dad talks to my wife, the way he did last time, I'll tell the sheriff on him and *you*. And if I ever see Nelle with cuts like yours on her body, anywhere on Nelle, I'll do more than tell the sheriff.

I laughed. I clapped my hand over my mouth.

—What would you do, Fred? Please tell me.

—I would blow up the church.

—You would?

Fred wasn't kidding, Nelle. Your dad was a psychopath. I studied his face. There was nothing. His face showed only calm. His jaw was set, his eyes fixed on the floor. He'd stated a threat. He would blow up the church. Now I wanted to see whether I could get him to elaborate, whether I could get the plan to solidify in his mind. If we'd failed to kill him with our shenanigans, here was an opportunity to cause some real damage. Maybe he wouldn't actually die, but with the church destroyed and Fred in jail, you and I could finally escape.

How many cuts would I have to give you? I didn't want to hurt you, Nelle, only create enough evidence to trigger his promised response. I struggled to hold in the quaver of excitement in my voice. His words, our plan taking shape, came as a wonderful shock.

—Would you blow it up at night? Or in the daytime?

—Doesn't matter. So long as you and your dad and everybody was inside.

—Did Christmas come early? I rubbed my hands, imitating him. —I'd really *love* to see you blow up my dad's church, Fred. That would be awesome. Please blow us all up, Fred.

—You think I'm lying.

—If I said I don't, would *you* think I'm lying?

He shook his head and wiped his nose. We never found out if he'd snorted any of the cocaine the Alejandro Brothers had stashed in the hollowed-out piano, but I wouldn't have been surprised if he'd done a line or two. Fred acted like he was on drugs.

I mean, I *know* cocaine's supposed to make you all hyper and chatty, but what if the special batch they'd hidden in the Baldwin produced the opposite effect? What if it slowed your speech and made you methodical and calm?

Fred had a calm mind. I don't have a calm mind. There was a lot going on under the surface in his dungeon with us talking about bombs and my dad and blowing up churches. Humor, sarcasm, seriousness. Fred wanted to say more, I sensed. He wanted to confess enough to get both of us in trouble, or not. He wanted to kill us all, or he wanted to divulge the kind of secret that forces you into staying in a room with a weird person you don't like.

Honestly, I don't know what he wanted. Sorry, Nelle, I didn't like your dad. I still wondered about his eyebrow bandage, and his body odor grossed me out. He smelled like Fritos and lunchmeat. Like how our cafeteria would smell after sixth period.

THAT ONE IS ON ME

I never heard Fred call the studio his "dungeon." I don't know where she got that. "Cafeteria" sounds about right. Of course, I only smelled him at his worst on stage when he was striking all our equipment. I guess his studio did not ventilate. Compared to Lester Hargreve, Fred Valenkemp smelled like a sweet angel covered in Johnson's baby powder. Like frankincense and myrrh, maybe.

She never said she killed him. I only heard her say, "He needed to go."

Which could mean anything, really. Elizabeth's an innocent girl going through some real trauma, hence her letters to Nelle from Warm Springs which I intercept—to understand her depressed mind. That night on South Padre Island, before I threw myself into the ocean, I yearned for a moment of clarity with my Elizabeth. As you've noticed by now, she can be a tough cookie. Why couldn't we have one honest fireside chat before a man went for a swim?

Also, if any notion of self-murder crossed my mind—if anything resembling the sinful act of suicide entered my highly tolerant mind, my body fought against it the moment I hit the cold waves. My reasons for jumping in had more to do with my alcohol-induced bravado than with my shame, but my shame is nothing compared to what my daughter's going through right now with her unravelling of this trauma regarding Fred, who is dead, okay?

You hear how I'm working her story into mine? That's how Jesus works in us. He unites us. He enfolds our hearts together until we become One Heart beating with His love.

I'd had an AK-47 stuck in my face. I'd allowed Lester to allow the Alejandro Brothers to store drugs in my church. I'd relapsed. I'd gone on a bender. I'd built a fire. I'd tried to have a talk with my daughter.

I took a bite of a stale piece of bread. A dip in the ocean seemed like nothing compared to what I'd already suffered. Compared to what *Jesus* suffered?

Elizabeth has me eating bread and shouting at the Lord to defend me against demons. Okay, I remember it a bit differently. I realize I have slim credibility at this point after I'd downed a twelve-pack of cheap beer. Let's not split hairs, though. I do remember telling her I got lost along the way. I admitted I didn't raise her the way a father should.

—I didn't raise you proper, Elizabeth. That one's on me.

—Whatever, Dad. I'm going for a walk.

With the wind blowing and the fire crackling, I may not have heard her say she was going for a walk. I should have been paying more attention. I may not have heard the disappointment in her voice after I'd talked my head off. I may have picked up a piece of the fire and carved "adonai"* in the sand, but Lourna didn't mention anything the next morning about a maverick log of firewood, not to mention letters erased or smeared by tide, so I have my doubts.

—My Lord, I'm starving. Is that bread? No, I asked Jesus for help. Jesus said you're on your own, buddy. You sang your songs for the afflicted, but you filled yourself with pride. You ignored your wife, your daughter. Also, you broke your promise. No chemical substances.

Go confront the cold deadness of the sea and report back to me.

Here's what I can report. I spoke with medical professionals about my daughter. Her guidance counselor and her psychiatrist discouraged me—sorry, Lourna—they discouraged *us* from using the word "commit." If I said she tried to "commit suicide," "commit" sounded stigmatizing and packed with moral judgment that risked further alienating the individual who had tried, attempted to "die by suicide" or "take her own life."

Like I said in the Preface, I'm not going back to correct any slips of the tongue.

---

* Sorry, Liz. No *way* I was sober enough to carve the letters right-to-left in the original Hebrew.

In any case, what the medical professionals said doesn't apply to my desire to run at the waves and dog-paddle my way to Florida. I wasn't suicidal. I was creating trauma in the mind of a person (my daughter) about to cut herself and become violently suicidal. Madness, depression, psychosis, whatever you might have—suicide will go along for the ride. It chooses. It's not a choice, or any single moment. It happens over time.

AND NOW A BRIEF WORD FROM OUR SPONSOR

Dear Nelle, My *Encyclopaedia Britannica* doesn't say anything about inertia and gravity creating two bulges of water at opposite ends of the globe. I'm missing the volume on "tides," "t" occurring near the end of the alphabet. I'm up to "l" for "lunar" or "lunatic." I do remember from science class that despite these two crazy "bulges" of water, gravity and inertia remain in relative balance over the rest of the Earth. Could you double-check with Mrs. Griffin?

THE UNDER TOAD RESCUED ME, NOT JESUS

Y'all mind if I say something directly to her on the air?

Liz, sweetheart. You read *The Awakening* in Honors English this semester. Proud of you. What did you make of the ending? You left out some crucial details. Weren't you disturbed by Pontellier's unholy pursuit of adultery and her so-called "freedom" from motherhood? She takes up painting. She doesn't want to hang with her kids. She swims off the coast of Grand Isle to the point of exhaustion. Do you agree with her "final act"? You never wrote about it one way or the other. Would you define her drowning as an act of triumph?

You deserved better than a B-minus. Too much plot summary? That English lady doesn't know what she's talking about. Heck, I would've given you an A. Keep up the good work!

Meanwhile, off the dark coast of South Padre Island: The waves pounded my stomach, my legs, and feet. The entire lower half of my body went numb. The waves broke stronger than the waves at Grand Isle. Stronger than the winds Aeolus ties up for Odysseus in a bag of oxhide leather, but probably not as strong as the ones that sweep over the sea Jesus crosses in a boat with his disciples, in Mark 4.35, where He falls asleep in the stern with his head on a pillow. ("Shouldn't we wake him up?" "How can he sleep with the storm about to capsize us?" "Does he realize we're all gonna die?") The waves of South Padre might have calmed if I'd listened to Jesus. I'd given up on Jesus. He hadn't given up on me.

The riptide swept under me, and the sand dissolved under my icy toes. My feet lost their hold on the sand floor, and waves crashed over my head. My ears and nose and mouth filled with saltwater. The sea lice that like to hide in the seaweed stung my neck. The undertow, what Elizabeth used to call the "Under Toad," God bless her heart, dragged me to the oil tankers.

One giant wave with the strength of Holyfield, the Real Deal, reared back and— Speaking of Holyfield, I heard y'all are gonna broadcast his fight against Riddick Bowe for the championship title next week? Bowe doesn't stand a chance. Holyfield will knock him out in the second round. I'll put money on Holyfield. One hundred dollars. No idle prophesy.

One haymaker of a wave reared back and battered the side of my head, KO'd me to the ocean floor, where I kissed the coral canvas and sank into a bed of sand. In other words, I got concussed. I couldn't think or see. How did I arise from my watery grave? It wasn't Jesus who lifted me off the ocean floor, I can tell you right now. It was the Under Toad.

SOMETHING CALLED RELIEF

Nelle, you actually believe his memory of my saying "Under Toad" saved him? Was it like some kind of epiphany that woke him from the watery depths of despair? Life waiting for him on the shore? How can you have a memory if you're knocked unconscious? And what's so special about my cute little toddler misspeak? Kids say dumb things all the time.

Next thing you know, he'll claim my saying "water mountain" at the McNay Art Museum instead of "water fountain" dissuaded him from divorcing Mom. Like he was pondering the futility of their relationship and stood on the verge of throwing in the towel, but heard me say "jag water" instead of "jaguar" when we were at the zoo and he said to himself, "How precious. The munchkin said 'jaguar.' She deserves a nice two-parent household. I'll give Lourna another chance." Words matter, I realize, but let's not get wacko here.

Honestly, they should have corrected my speech sooner—I needed to grow up fast so our family could have at least one adult to manage our affairs—or sent me to speech therapy before the kids I home-schooled with had a chance to make fun of me.

Ever feel like walking forever, Nelle, until the skin falls off your feet and your bones sink into the ground? That's how I felt the night my dad left his clothes piled by the fire and jumped into the waves. Not like I cared if he abandoned me or anything.

When I told him I was going for a walk, I wanted to walk forever.

The cold sand burned my bare feet. Too dark to see much. I stayed close to the water where only the outline of the surf in the moonlight remained visible, and the tide raced forward in thin sheets with their edges bubbling foam. By staying near the water, you avoid stepping on all the crap that washes up on our lovely Texas shores. The man-owars, the dead fish, spiky driftwood, barnacled rope, casting nets with rusty fish hooks, tar balls.

Teens who cut themselves are either looking to release anxiety or they're trying to feel something that's absent. I'm not sure which reason it was for me, Nelle. After my walk on the beach, my legs got tired and I turned around. We returned to Salterra the next morning.

At first, neither Lourna nor Zach spoke in the car. Like they didn't want to acknowledge his drunken behavior, or they'd moved past it without my awareness. They hardly fought when I was little, but now, after what he did—his abandonment deserved a fight. At least they could've screamed at each other like normal parents.

Nothing. Hours of outrageous silence went by. I put on my headphones and turned up the volume all the way thinking Zach would say you'd better turn it down or you're gonna go deaf. Or Lourna would turn in her seat and say sweetheart, your ears, and make the pinching motion with her thumb and forefinger, which would signal for me to dial it down.

Nothing. Nada. Zilch.

I got tired of the mix tape I'd made for the trip to the beach. I'd listened to both sides of the tape—Nirvana, Soundgarden, Mother Love Bone, Alice in Chains, 7 Year Bitch—but the singers were still singing the same songs and screaming the same way, and I felt like the music should have changed by now. I'd changed. Even "Come Bite the Apple" sounded too cheery, too glib, and since my grunge mix didn't mirror my new state of stifled fury, I was betrayed by the very bands I'd always trusted to channel my rage. Thanks, Kurt. Thanks, Chris. Thanks, Andrew. Thanks, Layne. Thanks, Stefanie. It's not happening.

I hit the stop button on my Walkman. Took off my headphones. Cracked the window. The highway played a loop of ocean surf in my head. The air on the horizon filled with plumes of white smoke from the toxic pollutants pouring out of oil refineries in the distance.

I tried to sleep, hoping to make the drive go faster, but every now and then I would experience a stab of pain in my leg, in the center of my left thigh. I don't know why. I'd sit upright and stare at my parents, Zach and Lourna, holding hands across the center console, and in my mind I'd accuse them of piercing me. They'd stuck me with a safety pin or a sewing needle while I had my eyes closed. Years ago, in summer camp, I'd learned to see with my eyelids closed. I mean someone looking at me would *think* I had my eyes closed, but I could see them. A thin blade of the visible world flickered around the pink center of my nose.

Like watching an old silent movie, only my world had color.

I did this trick for several minutes in the car, watching my thigh. When the pain returned and nobody's hand shot down to my thigh with a knife or any sharp object, I thought I was going crazy. Then I focused on the pain. It was brief but intense. I felt good.

After the first couple of times, I got over the pain and concentrated only on the relief that followed, and now I found myself waiting and eager for the stab of pain to happen again. When it didn't, I honestly grew frustrated, like what the heck was happening to my body?

I hadn't asked for this tiny stab of pain, but now that I wanted it, it wouldn't happen. The longer I waited, the more irritated and impatient I became. Finally, I asked Lourna if she had a pair of scissors. She couldn't hear me. She was talking to Zach. They still held hands, and they were talking in an animated way and listening to a radio show at the same time.

—Mom, can I borrow your makeup bag? *Mom*!

I knew she'd have nail clippers, or at least a pair of tweezers, and the desire to stab myself in the thigh became so intense I was ready to reach over the console, grab her purse, seize her makeup bag, and yank out the first piece of sharp metal I could find and do it right there in front of her. I nudged the back of her seat. She turned in slow motion.

—What, sweetheart?

—Can I borrow your makeup bag?

The paisley bag materialized in the space above the console. Lourna kept her attention on Zach, who talked about Watershed, how "his secret plan," or whatever, might work. He would simply "grow the church." We would grow as a family.

The way he kept saying "grow" made me think of a tumor.

—Sweetheart, Lourna said to me, please don't open the lipstick. It'll melt.

—Like I'd ever put on your heinous brown lipstick.

—It's not brown, sweetheart. It's toasted almond.

Her bag smelled like sunscreen and cotton candy from a melted tube of ChapStick. I found two nickels held together like an Oreo with a cough lozenge, also softened from the heat of the Texas sun.

In the side pocket I found a pair of nail clippers with a slide-out nail file, the point of which curved like a shark's tooth. I inhaled a deep breath of the cotton candy air. I swung the file into knife position, closing the compound lever so the file pointed straight at the back of Zach's seat. Thankfully the file had a sharp point. Sharp enough for my purpose.

The problem would be to keep the file from sliding sideways in my hand when I jabbed the point into my thigh, attempting to recreate the beautiful mystery pain I'd experienced moments earlier, so I decided I'd go for it, the way a woman might jab a key into a man's eyes if he tried to sexually assault her in a dark parking lot, and go for it I would—I would slam the point into the center of my thigh with enough of a crushing downward force to break the skin. First I wiped the grit off the tip of the file. Whatever crud Lourna had scraped out from under her fingernail I didn't want injected into my bloodstream.

—I wouldn't use your lipstick for a thousand dollars.

The point met its target, and I clenched my jaw to keep from screaming.

Outrageous. Silence.

—Elizabeth. Lourna turned to retrieve the makeup bag she loved more than her daughter. —You're bleeding. Honey, she's bleeding. Sweetheart, what *happened*?

—It's fine. I'm okay, Mom.

After the wave of pain crested, relief broke over me and fled through my body. I definitely felt something. The balloon in my brain popped, and a sweet hiss of air escaped. My eyes brimmed. I couldn't wait to do it again.

BALLOON IN THE BRAIN

Hold up. My daughter said *what* about her illness? Sorry. Parables I understand. Metaphors, usually. "Balloon in the brain"? Never heard this one before. Also, I was driving us home from the beach. Tired and hungover. A bad headache. Took everything in me to keep my eyes on the road. So—she wanted to "feel something" by hurting herself and hurting the people around her who cared about her the most. Okay. I still can't wrap my head around the second part, but we're working through this. How was I supposed to help her if she wouldn't talk to me?

Before she grew up and got so complicated and lippy, I would hold her in my arms and she'd stay quiet for hours. Okay. Maybe not hours. Two hours. One good solid hour. Enough time to change her diaper, grab her bottle from the fridge, and rock her on the porch at our house in San Antonio before she let out a single whimper. And during services at New Foundations. People said we were so lucky. She sleeps through the night. She never cries unless she's in real pain or got a soiled diaper or if one of the legs on the animal balloon the clown gave her at the birthday party pops and shrivels against its inflated body. These were all obvious, easy problems. Ball of vanilla ice cream falls off the cone onto the hot sidewalk? Buy her another ice cream. Tail of her monkey balloon pops and withers? Make her another monkey, Mr. Clown.

Preteen Elizabeth would lead us in prayer at meals, and once she appeared on stage at New Foundations to bless the offering. We're talking a crowd of four thousand with a service broadcast across the United States and several foreign nations. Good measure, pressed down, shaken together. The Hembreys gave and *for*gave. Never once doubted she could handle the responsibilities of Assistant of Youth

Ministries at Watershed. With the group lessons at Freedom Keys, the Lock-in, Popcorn Movie Night, Thanksgiving Dinner—with all the extra activities, she did amazing work. It's possible I gave her too much work. What did she mean by the "balloon in my brain"? What was inside? Stress? Sadness? Anger? Why couldn't she talk to us about her feelings? She could *talk* to people. God had awesome plans for her. I blew it. I blew up the balloon in her brain. She went looking for other ways to make it pop.

NOT BEGINNING TO SEE THE LIGHT

After South Padre, I didn't know if Lourna forgave Zach, or if Zach forgave Lourna, or if Lourna needed to hear Zach forgive himself. Were they staying together? Was she leaving him?

If not, why not? What happened?

I needed one of these two children to explain, but in order to talk to them I would have to acknowledge their existence. In my view, acknowledging their existence meant I forgave them, which I didn't, and by talking to them I'd have to recognize them as my parents again, which I didn't. They were Zach and Lourna.

The pain I experienced in the car didn't last, but I delighted in the pain.

The garage door grumbled open and Zach rolled us inside. The floor of our car was covered in sand and the tissues Lourna had given me to stop the bleeding. I let them believe the cut was an accident, or they assumed I was bored and wanted to test boundaries, cross a threshold, or whatever. Like after a nosebleed or a menstrual accident, blood-stained Kleenex littered the floor. And sand. The sight of my blood didn't fascinate me.

—Let's go inside, Zach said. —We'll unload later. Do we still have ice?

He wouldn't have to go far to check the freezer. Our house was the size of a coffin. Two bedrooms and one bathroom with uneven plank flooring. Nelle, you should have seen how we lived in San Antonio. We had a computer. We had a car phone. I had my own bathroom with a sink and bathtub, nice tiles. Before I learned water can kill you, I would fill the giant tub—back then we had an enormous hot-water heater in a two-car garage—pour shampoo and soak for hours. Sorry, I won't mention the San Antonio house again, makes me sad.

No ice in the freezer. The trays were empty. Zach found a bag of frozen peas, lay on the couch, placed the peas on his forehead, and sighed. I went to my room. It had a musky stench, as if my P.E. uniform had jumped out of the hamper and danced around while I was gone. I'm sure he'll tell you about the "headless cockroach" he saw in the warehouse, but when I turned on the lights in my bedroom, a roach did run across the floor and disappeared under my dresser.

Roaches didn't frighten me, and I could not have cared less about the roach in my bedroom. I was focused on my immediate goal. I wanted to cut myself to feel the relief again.

The door to our only bathroom had a cheap barrel lock like something you'd see at a gas station, so we'd instituted a knock-first policy: If you find the door closed, you knock first before opening it *even if you don't think anyone's inside, Zach*. Which is what he forgot to do before he tried to shoulder his way into the bathroom while I sat on the toilet seat with his razor blade held several inches above my thigh.

—Hey, hold on. I'm *in* here!

—Sweetheart? My dad's voice boomed. —You okay?

I heard him breathing on the other side of the door.

—I'm fine. Can I have some privacy, please?

The creaking of his footsteps receded as he returned to his nest in the living room. I heard him whisper to Lourna, but I didn't catch what he said. I'd found his razor in the top right-hand drawer, lying on a hand towel, a straight blade with a handle cut from the horn of a foraging animal, like a deer or elk. Zach had inherited the razor from his father. I know it sounds weird, but the razor and I became instant friends. I named it "friend." I never said "friend" out loud. I didn't want people to think I was crazy.

One time I had a nightmare where our house got broken into and the only stuff the robbers took were Lourna's jewelry and my friend. The robbers left a rabbit's foot keychain in its place. I don't know what this means. Dreams aren't supposed to make sense. But I woke up in a panic. I raced into the bathroom and my heart did not slow until I squeezed the antler handle in my hand to make sure my friend had not been stolen.

Now I stared at the razor while I sat on the toilet seat. The blade wasn't clean. A smudge of dried shaving cream and tiny bits of black stubble showed on the polished silver. I wondered how often Zach used the heirloom. I wiped the blade with the towel. I chose a place higher up on my thigh where I could hide the cut under my shorts. Instead of applying the blade to my skin with a gentle downward stroke, like you would if you were actually going to shave, I pressed the end corner of the blade into my skin at a ninety-degree angle.

I held the blade for a few seconds, bit my lips, and lifted my chin toward the ceiling. Relief followed the wave of agony, and my eyes watered. When I released the pressure of the blade, I bled. I grabbed a wad of toilet paper and held it against the cut, counted to forty-eight, and the bleeding stopped. My blood clotted well. I promised my friend for Lent I'd give up all blood thinners like ginger, aspirin, cayenne peppers (which I liked), almonds (which I also liked even though they hurt my teeth), garlic, cinnamon (also a tough one), and turmeric, which we never ate anyway. Lourna thought Indian food could trigger a migraine.

I took better care of my friend than Zach did. I didn't want to get caught. I hid the cuts and the pain, and I did well for a few days until we went to the lake.

BACK TO PREACHING LIKE NOTHING HAPPENED

She'll say I pretended nothing happened, but my near drowning in the Gulf of Mexico restored my faith in God, if I did temporarily lose it, which I'm not quite ready to admit. I returned to preaching the gospel with a renewed sense of purpose. Yes, I included the story of Jonah in my sermons, and I'll talk about him again when we get around to the Thanksgiving dinner this year. I think there's a great lesson when Jonah says he "will sacrifice to You with the voice of thanksgiving." I will not remind y'all how, during the meal, the fish vomited Jonah onto dry land. Like I said, we're gonna get the temperatures of the birds right this time, I promise.

Volunteers, y'all sign up early. We're expecting a full house.

Yes, I brought up my near drowning during my first sermon after South Padre. No, I left out the drinking and Elizabeth piercing herself with my wife's cuticle pusher. (I didn't know for sure she'd done it on purpose.) Plus, the details didn't fit with the details of my sermon. Noah wasn't a drunk. Plus, I'd already preached more or less about my debauchery from the days I wrote meaningless jingles for commercials. The redemption story had been told.

I returned from South Padre, tired and in need of the Holy Spirit. Lourna and I were falling in love again. I preached love. I preached the ocean. I preached the sacred waters to purify the spirit. John baptized Jesus with water. The baptism signified the Holy Spirit pouring out over everybody's flesh, which my daughter thinks is kind of gross, but don't listen to her. She's trying to take your eye off the ball. This is change, renewal, rebirth.

I bought a horse trough. I put it on stage and filled it with water. The first time we attempted to baptize someone in the horse trough, the water was too cold, so I bought this heating device. It was the size of a hair dryer and I dangled it into the trough. Fred nearly had a heart attack when he saw all that water next to his fancy electric gear.

—Pastor, you sure this is safe? There's a lot of juice up here.

—All is well, my brother, I said. All is well.

I had so much faith in Jesus. Wish I could've baptized myself. Had Watershed been struck by lightning, Jesus would've protected us. Returned from the teeth of the Mighty Tempest, I promise you a little water in a horse trough can't hurt you. I should've said this to Fred. He looked real worried, and angry at me, as we prepared our first baptism.

The first one was a girl around Elizabeth's age. I can't use her real name on the air. She wore a pair of jeans and a flannel shirt under the white baptismal robe. I don't have to explain the reasons for proper attire under the robe during and after immersion.

You wouldn't believe what some folks put on (or forget to put on) under their robes.

After my Prayer Partners lowered her into the trough, I asked the girl why she'd submitted to the rite of Holy Baptism. I stuck my microphone in her face. I wanted all of Watershed to hear her beautiful words. Fred gathered the slack in the microphone cord to make sure none of it touched the trough or the hair-dryer thing floating in the water.

—Because I've accepted Jesus Christ as my personal Lord and Savior, the girl said. Everybody applauded, the band started playing "Jesus in the Center," and we lifted her out of the trough. A little water spilled onto the blue tarp I'd placed under the trough.

I wish Fred had been more moved by the Holy Spirit the way the rest of us were during the Watershed baptism. I also wish Elizabeth had been more attentive. She was supposed to be back in the office with a towel and blow dryer for the girl. It gets cold in Watershed.

HOW WATER CAN KILL YOU

Water puddled on the blue tarp, but luckily none spread onto the stage. Fred would've had a heart attack. The girl had taken off her glasses before she'd gotten into the horse trough. Funny how Zach left out that part of the ceremony. This girl they baptized was totally blind without her glasses. Her parents feared they'd fall off and get lost during her immersion, so they asked Pastor Zacharias to take off her glasses and put them somewhere safe. I saw him put her glasses on top of one of the monitors on stage. I remembered the glasses. He didn't.

After the baptism, the girl's mother shouted, Your *glasses!*

Of course the girl couldn't hear her mother over Fred's keyboards and everybody singing "Jesus in the Center." Anyway, how do you expect a legally blind girl to find her glasses? What's she supposed to do? Fumble around on stage and grope the carpet with her fingers? During all the excitement, Zach couldn't remember where he'd put them. During the baptism, until I found them, this girl couldn't see a thing.

Did I mention water can kill you? And by "kill you," I don't mean "kill your soul," or "ruin your spirit" like how Medieval Christians outlawed public bathing after they thought it led to immoral behavior like heavy petting and sex. I mean there's drowning, and the toxic particles floating freely in water that can kill you. If enough poison seeps into your pores, you'll die.

This is well documented.

Look it up in *Encyclopaedia Britannica* if you don't believe me. If you're concerned about having a stench, it's no big deal, you get a rag or a small towel. Spray some perfume on it. Tranquility, whatever. The brand doesn't matter. Spray the rag with perfume, rub whatever body parts you want cleaned, and shake on some Johnson's baby powder.

It doesn't have to be Johnson's, but I prefer Johnson's. Dash the powder on your skin and spread it around with your fingers. The perfume will keep you smelling nice, and the baby powder will block your pores and protect you and keep out the moisture that can put lethal diseases into your body like cancer.

Avoiding water is like putting on your seatbelt. It takes very little effort but if you don't do it on a regular basis the consequences are huge.

I didn't know the truth about water until Fred told me. Explained it in his weird-but-true way. The secret he passed on, the thing he thought would unite us, turned out to be the reason he needed to go. But it's late, Nelle. They're turning off the lights at Warm Springs. I was going to tell you about Salterra Lake. It'll have to wait until tomorrow.

HEAVEN REST US, I AM NOT ASBESTOS

I believe I'm beginning to understand the origins of this crazy belief of hers about water. It begins with my night in the ocean, so if I can steer us back to South Padre for a moment.

The riptide dragged me beyond the second sand bar. I couldn't stand. A wave knocked me to the ocean floor, where I scraped my forehead on a piece of coral. I came up with blood pouring out of my forehead, the wound throbbing. Saltwater stung my face. I couldn't see much of anything. Blood and saltwater poured into my eyes. I didn't have time to worry about sharks. I swung my arms and legs at the churning sea and stuck my mouth above the surface in intervals long enough to inhale deep gulps of air before a wave knocked me under again.

I wasn't anyone special or anointed down there. Yes, the Lord had sent a great wind over the sea, but I didn't consider myself Jonah, nor did I believe the Lord had chosen to punish me for drinking twelve beers. I was a human fighting for survival. Plain and simple.

The mind sabotages the body. The mind says stay down, give up, the lot has fallen on you, let the tidal forces sweep your body into the abyss. The body knows better. I didn't see my life "flash before my eyes," nor did I see any "tunnels of light" or "angel reaching for me." Not saying it can't happen, the angels and tunnels of light. Only, I experienced no vision.

The Bible says, "Heaven and earth will pass away, but His words will not pass away." I wished His words would've stuck with me instead of the perfume jingle I'd written ten years earlier. I was drowning, and the earworm of an awful perfume ad stuck in my head. Is it possible to die with bad lyrics stuck in one's head? Lyrics not even worth printing, in my opinion. Not like the ones in "I Won't Dance," by Jerome Kern, if that's what Elizabeth means by assigning me the title at the beginning of this chapter. Maybe I *am* asbestos.

Is it possible that no flash of light, no tunnel of light, no chorus of angels blowing trumpets will greet us as our short sleep begins and Christ awakens us to Immortality, but a phrase like "for the woman on the go, for the woman with ability…"? Possible this would play through our minds? Or a random series of pictures? Objects as mundane as cow manure?

A couple of things I did see while drowning in the Gulf of Mexico:

The rescue ship in *The Raft of Medusa*, an oil painting by Théodore Géricault. I saw the tiny sailboat on the horizon in the painting, a dark speck of paint. I saw a perfume bottle from the commercial with the jingle I'd written, only this bottle was empty, and its bulb sprayer stuck out from the silver lid like a small black microphone. And of course I heard the jingle. The earworm crawled into my head. I saw a manuscript page from a Beethoven sonata where the broken notes rise up from the bottom of the page and crash against and around the ones that descend from the top of the page. The notes reminded me of the waves. I always wanted to be a prophet who witnessed Grand Visions. Meanwhile, panic screamed in my mind. I'd have rather seen the face of my wife and daughter, the two women I'd left on the island, but instead I saw these random pictures and I heard this horrible perfume ad replaying in my mind.

I didn't think I was going to see Lourna and Elizabeth again.

The Raft of the Medusa, oil on canvas by Théodore Géricault, c. 1819.

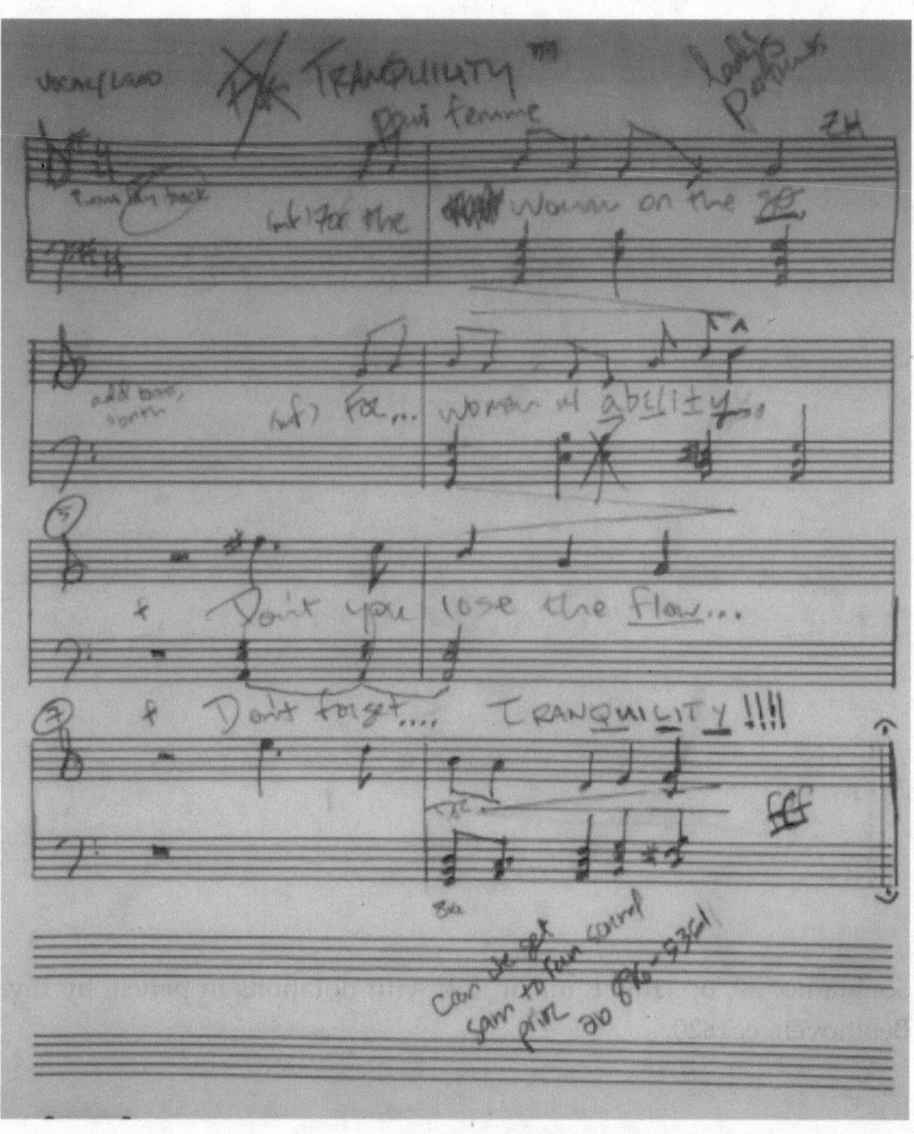

pour femme, pencil on staff paper by Zach Patrick Hembrey, c. 1979.

Sonata no. 30, op. 109, E major, ink with notations in pencil, by L.v. Beethoven, c. 1820.

LITURGICAL DETERGENT:
STILL NOT TALKING ABOUT THE LAKE

According to my *Encyclopaedia Britannica,* Beethoven's Sonata in E major was written in 1820. One year earlier, Géricault shocked the French world by painting what he considered a realistic depiction of a shipwreck's aftermath. Abandoned by their captain who ordered the rope towing their raft to be cut, severing their lifeline, the lower-rank soldiers drifted for thirteen days. Fifteen of the original one hundred forty-seven men survived. They endured starvation, dehydration, delusions, madness. They ate the flesh of their fallen brethren. I say "brethren" instead of "mates" to project a Christian slant Géricault may not have wanted, but whatever.

I'm writing this for my dad, the pastor.

When you think about it, anything can become liturgical. One hundred and seventy-three years after Géricault gave artistic form to his obsession with dead people, you and I poured Palmolive into Fred's bottle of peach schnapps, hoping he'd drink the soap. We didn't go far enough, Nelle. I poured in liquid Tide detergent, but antifreeze would've been better. We left the adulterated coffee on Fred's desk in his studio. We know he survived our attempts to poison him.

He died at Watershed Church at the end of Franklin Road.

We forgive the sin of the cannibals in Géricault's painting by applying the analogy of Christ's offering in Matthew 26.26-8: "While they were eating, Jesus took a loaf of bread, and after blessing it he broke it, gave it to the disciples, and said, 'Take, eat; this is my body.' Then he took a cup, and after giving thanks he gave it to them saying, 'Drink from it, all of you; for this is my blood of the covenant, which is poured out for many for the forgiveness of sins.'"

Before Jesus rode into Jerusalem on a donkey to celebrate the Passover, Mary bathed his feet with an expensive perfume. Probably more expensive than Tranquility. Using her hair as a brush, she spread the perfume across the top of Jesus' feet. Judas and some of the other disciples considered the gesture wasteful. "We should've sold the perfume and given the money to the poor," Judas said. Jesus said to the betrayer, "Leave her alone. She's saving the rest for my funeral rites. You'll always have the poor, but you won't always have me."

In 1979, Zach wrote commercial ad music for Tranquility. The perfume company paid him good money. The chief priests paid Judas thirty pieces of silver for betraying Jesus to them. After Zach wrote the ad, and others, and after he blew his money on Bohemia and Kaniché rum, he would wake in the mornings with severe hangovers. During the hangovers, he would lie on the couch with a bag of frozen peas on his forehead and try to remember his purpose in life.

During this time, Zach believed someone or something had betrayed him.

—I feel betrayed, Zach probably told himself. I've achieved everything I set out to accomplish, I'm living the American Dream, I've written successful jingles for very important corporations, for which I'm generously compensated. I own a nice house, no mortgage, I have a beautiful wife and daughter, all the Kaniché I can drink, and yet... I'm empty. If someone had told me my life would turn out this empty, I'd have said no thanks. And yet here I am, taking their money, saying thank you, thank you, and why don't I feel truly grateful? Why can't I relax? Moreover, why can't I perceive the betrayal that consumes me? Have my ears closed up? Have my eyes gone dim? Why don't I have the words to describe what has betrayed me?

It would take many years and many prayers before he found a language to describe the betrayal. Jesus said I am the Way. Jesus forgave him and told him the only person Zach had betrayed was himself. Everyone has a talent, Jesus said to him, and you can't bury your talent in greed and waste. If you hide your talent in the ground, you will die. Your talent lies elsewhere in playing music, but also in preaching the Holy Book. Jesus said the eye is the lamp of the body. If your eyes are good, your whole body will be full of light. Right now your eyes are bad, all you see is the evil around you, and you have filled your whole body with darkness. You think your life's all wrapped up nice like a burrito, but your burrito life hasn't started yet. It's just a tortilla, no meat, let alone beans and cheese. Zach, my friend, you need to get up off the couch. Follow me. Open your eyes to the Light. Forgive yourself and don't give up the truth of what makes you great, your Faith in Me. Faith, Truth, and Beauty shall turn your songs into sweet Gospel, and no longer shall your soul be a formless void.

In San Antonio one morning I was still too young to remember, Zach rolled off the couch and pulled on some nice clothes and in a simple voice told his family to get ready, they were going to church. We went to New Foundations. Zach got Saved.

—What else do you read besides the Bible? Rachel asked me while we were watching the girls swim in the lake. We'd found a picnic table in the shade. Squirrels darted across the brittle grass. Sparrows chirped in the branches of the oak trees over our heads.

—St. Augustine. C.S. Lewis. I like watching Longhorns football. I didn't go to UT for college, I went to Tech, but I was hoping Elizabeth would go. Everybody we knew in San Antonio seemed to be a Longhorns fan. They'd ship their kids straight up I-35.

—And now you're in Aggie country.

—That's right. I don't understand. We're closer to Austin than College Station.

—It's not about distance. People out here feel more connected to the land. There's more to learn at College Station about farming and agriculture than in Austin.

—You're from Houston. How'd you get this insight?

—By looking around. It's nice out here.

—Yeah, last time we went to a lake like this Elizabeth was two. She had a fever the whole time and threw up in the car. Still, watching the glassy water. Not a single boat out. Glorious. I'd never been happier in my life.

—You do that a lot, you know.

—What?

—Talk about how Elizabeth was when she was a baby.

—We're working through our issues.

—Have you been listening to her?

—Oh, sure. I'm getting silence.

—Did she make those cuts on her leg herself?

—Yes.

I winced as I lifted the watermelon out of the cooler. Nelle had made a face at Elizabeth when she took off her shorts by the lake. The kind of reaction I'd been dreading. *Those cuts on her leg.* (Lourna and I knew about the cutting, but Elizabeth hadn't attempted any more outright violence against herself or others. The professionals we'd spoken to said self-harming didn't always lead to suicidal behavior. We were in an awful wait-and-see mode. We knew she needed help, but we worried our intervention might push her away.)

—Lourna said I shouldn't make a fuss, I told Rachel. Kids go through phases. Elizabeth's opening up more. I think she's coming around.

—That's not a phase. Rachel took the knife and sliced the watermelon. The two halves of watermelon opened on the table and juice from the red center dripped on the tablecloth.

—I can't believe Lourna told you not to make a fuss, Rachel said. If I found out Nelle was cutting herself, I'd make more than a fuss. Listen, y'all need to get her professional help.

—Yes, we're praying. Also, we might take her to Warm Springs.

—That's good, pastor. I hear Warm Springs provides excellent care. You should talk to her about it, prepare her for everything. I noticed you no longer speak to her like you're talking to our whole congregation. That's good, too.

—I get better results when we speak directly. I'm trying to ask more open-ended questions, otherwise I get a simple yes or no and a lot of silence. She knows how to kill a conversation. Like, Elizabeth, how do you *really* feel about Nelle's father?

—What did she say?

—Oh, nothing. She's keeping her cards close to her chest.

—But has she said anything else about Fred?

—I don't think so. Why? What're you getting at?

—Does she still think my husband is Satan?

I bit into a slice of watermelon, nodding. It was sweet, juicy. Seedless.

—I liked her story, Rachel said, about the hollow at the bottom of the lake.

During the car ride, Elizabeth had told Nelle at least once every ten years a kid goes missing from Salterra Lake. The girl will swim out too deep, she said, and this hollow, like a cave, sucks her down, and nobody can save her. —If you can hold your breath long enough, Elizabeth said, you might reach an air pocket, way down inside the hollow, but the current is too strong to swim back to the surface. Basically you have to live down there. Nelle asked what happens if you can't find an air pocket inside the hollow.

Elizabeth shrugged. —They've sent divers near the entrance, but no kid has ever come back. They say time passes differently under the lake. The only thing to eat is this moss that grows on the walls. It looks like cotton candy, but it tastes disgusting. The kids eat it anyway. They have nothing else. After a few weeks of eating the moss, they lose their sense of time, and they forget about their world up above on land.

They forget they ever lived above the lake. They forget they had families.

—Yes, I said to Rachel. My daughter's a creative one. Behind us was a field of brittle grass with fire ant hills, like little volcanos made of ash. —Hope she didn't scare Nelle.

—Nelle loves scary stories. Where'd you say your wife was?

I gazed past the girls splashing in the cove and squinted at the sunlight sparking off the waves as if Lourna were somewhere out there and I could summon her. —Oh, sunlight gives her headaches. We got back from a recent trip to the beach. She wasn't quite ready.

—I knew someone who was allergic to the sun.

—So Fred's in New York? (I tried to sound calm. I'd invited the Valenkemps, assuming Fred could make it. Rachel surprised me when she said he'd be out of town. She surprised me even more when she said she and her daughter would like to come anyway.)

—For the weekend, Rachel said. —His old buddy from their furniture-moving days, also a composer, they're debuting his rock symphony at the Brooklyn Academy of Music.

—Think I'll go get some more sunscreen from the car. I know they already put some on, but Lourna would be furious if Elizabeth got burned. Need anything?

Of course I remember the pep talk I'd given Fred on his audition day, how I'd told him God had greater plans for him than a New York debut, and now I wondered if Fred resented me for saying it. Would the sting of quitting too early hit him when he saw his friend's concert? Would Fred think, What if I'd stuck it out longer? What if I ignored that self-righteous pastor in Texas and returned to writing serious music? What are God's *real* plans for me?

—No, I'm good, Rachel said. I'll get lunch ready.

On my way to get the sunscreen, we crossed paths. The fisherman and I. He wore a trench coat over a flannel shirt with six or seven pockets, and a pair of waders. He carried two fishing poles with gold spoons flashing on the line. We may have waved or nodded hello.

I didn't get a close look at his face. For Elizabeth's sake, I wish I had.

THE HOLLOW AT THE BOTTOM OF THE LAKE

I didn't see Zach leave the picnic table. The lake had a small beach with a five-foot wall of limestone behind it. From the water, I could see the beach and picnic tables but not the field.

The sun warmed the upper layer of the lake, but several feet below a band of cold water gripped my skin. I dove into this layer of cold and grabbed some mud and gravel. Nelle, I wanted to shove the mud in your face, pull a prank, but when my hands broke the surface of the water, the sludge slipped away through my fingers.

I dove under again, and this time I held myself perfectly still with my knees crushed against my chest, and I floated sideways underwater. When I opened my eyes the water appeared in shades of yellow and green, a cosmos with the sun overhead clouded by the underside of the lake and the rays shining down in swift bands and the bubbles I'd made, kicking my way down and exhaling, swirling around me like exploding stars.

The bubbles that clung to the scars on my thighs were smaller. Underwater my cuts became ribbons of pink outfitted with silver beads. I held my breath and expanded my cheeks like a blowfish. How cool if the story I'd told you about the hollow at the bottom of the lake were true. I could have stayed down there forever. I felt a perch nibble my foot quick as a peck-kiss. I'd seen them before. These small fish, their bodies no bigger than a leaf, but I'd never felt one touch me. The nibble didn't hurt but it creeped me out. All the air came rushing out of my nose and mouth, and I kick-glided back to the surface. —How long was I under?

—I don't know, you said. —I wasn't counting.

—All right. You go. I'll count. You seemed reluctant until I put my hand on your shoulder and pushed. I watched you take a shallow breath and slide under. —One alligator, two alligator, three.... After twelve alligators, you came up gasping, pinching your nose.

—Something nibbled my thigh, you said.

—It was a snake, I said.

—Shut up. No, it wasn't.

—I'm serious. Cottonmouths swim in this lake. Everybody knows.

You became quiet, treading water. You looked back at the shore, your teeth chattered, and when you whipped your eyes towards mine I saw them widen with panic.

—My turn, I said, before you could object. —You count for me.

I took a big gulp of air and swam hard and kicked my body as far out as I could. I wanted to beat your record of twelve alligators. I wanted to make you think a snake grabbed me. I wanted to stay under until the way you looked at me when I took off my shorts no longer singed. I wanted to stay under until you believed I'd been swept down into the hollow.

Elizabeth means my chronology is off. She doesn't mean I left her in the lake and went to get sunscreen *at the wrong time*. And don't worry, folks, Lourna and I have one of those tax-exempt college funds I couldn't have drained for booze if I'd wanted to, which I didn't. And I'm glad she's already thinking about college at her age.

For the record, I did not relapse immediately after I spent the night in the warehouse. It took time. It took me and Rachel in the music room and me remembering what it was like to stand in front of a beautiful woman. So I did the obvious thing a man of faith would do: I went home to my *wife* and suggested we book a condo on South Padre Island.

Why couldn't I swat at the fruit flies?

I told you, folks. Lester's guys duct-taped my arms to the chair.

I'm calm. I don't need a glass of water. I'm good. Like I said, I'm not Beelzebub. Joseph? Ezekiel? Sure, I wanted to be a prophet. Pride kept me low. I could've been worse. I could have *known** Mrs. Valenkemp. What led y'all to think it happened? Because we talked at Lake Salterra? Can a man of God describe a woman's ankles without y'all thinking he's got a hidden motive? Sorry I lost the girl's glasses. I'm not an ophthalmologist.

Normally in this part of the service, we'll have a guest who wants to rapture. Some of our congregants do prefer the revival aspect of Christianity, and I wouldn't prohibit the Holy Spirit from moving inside anyone. I'm a practical man. It happens faster than you'd think. We're playing "Jesus I'll Never Forget," and the worshiper falls back

---

* yada' / יָדַע

into the arms of my Prayer Partners, usually two strong men, who catch the worshiper and lower him or her to the floor.

How long does the Holy Spirit move in the body of someone undergoing rapture? How long does the individual get to lie in front of my stage, smiling into heaven with his or her eyes closed? You'd think Jesus would decide. Unfortunately, this one's my call.

Last time, this lady in a scarlet dress waving a tambourine raptured—I'm not gonna name names; y'all know who I'm talking about—and remained on the floor all the way through "Jesus, I'll Never Forget," "Living in the River," and "My Soul's a Fire." I was saying the Benediction, blessing the crowd, and this lady still would not get up.

—Is she all right? I said into the microphone. I gave my Prayer Partners a look. They knew I was irritated. I mean, I'm not saying you can't rapture in my church, but if you're gonna lie there during the entire service, it's distracting for the folks who just want to sing and praise the Lord and get on with their Sunday.

I told Jesus, I said, I'm gonna put a time limit on rapturing.

—May the Lord bless you and keep you. I stared down at her and shook my head. I glanced at my Prayer Partners again. They knew what to do.

Ten minutes, folks. That's all you get for rapturing. Otherwise, it's too distracting, and we've got to get on with the show. The lady? Oh, she was fine. After they picked her up off the floor, she said praise Jesus and banged her tambourine and danced around.

Our band had stopped playing, but the Holy Music continued in her mind.

HE MEANS "OPTOMETRY": TRICKS OF THE EYE

Dear Nelle, Zach doesn't understand the difference between an ophthalmologist and an optometrist. Other than music and the Bible, he's pretty ignorant about people's jobs. You and I are not ignorant. Nor are we blind. You saw Fred jump into the lake. I don't blame you for not stopping him. I'm trying to show you why he needed to go.

What grabbed my ankle wasn't a fish. I knew it was the hand of a man, and I couldn't shake him loose. At the bottom of the lake, I had nothing to hold onto, no cypress roots, no plant roots, none of the slimy grass that grows in the shallows. I'd swum past the littoral zone.

Fred's hand took hold of my foot, his other hand clasped my ankle, and he yanked me out of the deep end. I thrashed and screamed for him to let me go. I clawed at his neck. I got water up my nose. I choked. I flipped onto my side and kicked him underwater. He grabbed me between the legs and squeezed. I couldn't breathe. He squeezed harder.

Fred dragged me up to the surface and scowled as if I could have slipped away. He spat his words in my ear. —Easy, he said. Easy. I saved you. You almost *died*.

—Let me go. I'm not drowning.

—They're talking again. Told you what would happen.

—Let me go, you freak.

—Still think I'm lying?

I was so ashamed, the way he carried me to the beach, and no one intervened. No one stopped him from squeezing me and dropping me onto the sand like a dead fish. Where were you, Nelle? Why didn't you come help me? Why did you and Rachel stand by while he pulled me out of the lake? Holy Mother of God. Y'all knew I didn't need his help.

—Easy. You're welcome.

—Get *away*.

After he touched me, I fell into a paralysis. My brain couldn't tell my arms or legs to move. My field of vision blurred and shrank. (I'm still on "l" for "littoral," "limnetic," "lunar," or "lunatic." What's after "limnetic"?) He'd attacked me in the limnetic zone and introduced me to the nightmare of possible future attacks. My legs collapsed. The cuts on my thigh, no longer underwater but still damp, puffed out like a pair of sunburned lips.

Particles in the water could penetrate the pores, infect, and kill. I could feel his thumbs pressing into me. I coughed up water and I sobbed, and not one of you moved. Nelle, you'd already gone up to the picnic table with your mom. I saw you tilt your head to the side and smack it to clear the water from your ear. Rachel held your flip-flops while you brushed the sand off your feet. Y'all didn't look down at the shore. Y'all didn't even look in my direction. Not one of you did a damn thing. I thought of what Jesus meant when he said "you will be betrayed even by parents and brothers, by relatives and friends."* He needed to go, Nelle.

Wherever I saw a drop of water on my skin I smeared it with my thumb as if it were a mosquito sucking my blood. I couldn't get my skin to dry fast enough.

—Dad, bring me a towel! Let's go home.

—What do we say to our new guests, folks?

Rachel dropped a towel onto my shoulders. —It's okay, honey. He didn't know.

Didn't know? Yada, yada, yada.

She wasn't talking about Zach. She meant *Fred*, her husband, who'd grabbed me. I grabbed the towel and dried myself off. Feet, shins, legs, stomach, armpits, arms, face, ears, hair. By the time I'd finished drying my hair, the towel was too wet. I threw it in the sand.

—Dad, I want to go *home!*

—What do we say to our new guests, folks?

Fred climbed out of the lake on the opposite side of the cove. All his wet clothes clung to his body, and his socks flapped like fins off the

* Luke 21.16.

ends of his toes. Rachel handed Fred the waders he'd left at the top of the steps, and it sounded like she was apologizing to him for my behavior. For *my* behavior? Are you kidding me? Then he took off. Fred grabbed his waders and ran back to the parking lot. Where was Zach? How could he leave me shivering by the lake?

Fred later told Zach he'd thought I was drowning and jumped in to save me, or whatever. Bull crap. Fred attacked me. If enough water invades your skin, you can die. Fred hadn't done what he'd promised. He needed to go. You and Rachel finally asked me if I was okay. I couldn't talk. So humiliated. None of y'all understood how ~~explored~~ exposed I felt. Zach has no problem being vulnerable. Under the cloak of Christianity he can jump on stage and shout about all his personal failures from the time before he found God, but I'm different. I don't have God.

Want to know how your dad got that cut above his eye? He'd attacked another girl, and she scratched him as she tried to defend herself. He must have.

I should've clawed Fred's eyes out. He needed to go. Before I left the beach, I turned toward the lake. Swirls of milky fluid drifted in the shallows. Either Zach had bought the cheap stuff, or we hadn't waited long enough. Our sunscreen polluted the water. We walked back to the car. I can't remember if anyone cleaned off the picnic table.

I'd have to become someone else. At the very least I'd need to change my name.

TRYING OUT NAMES FOR THE MUSIC SCHOOL

Lourna and I were always trying out names for the music school: Jesus Sings! Jesus Scales! Sopranos for Christ. Hymn and Her. Major Fugue. Presto-Manna. Jesus Trills. Spiritual Tempo. Freedom Notes. Freedom Beats. Jesus Beats. Holy Little Tenors. Holy Forte!

Etudes for Attitude. Spiritual Pitch. Opus Omegas.

Jehovah's Jig. Free from Sincopation.

We always went with "Freedom Keys," but I had my reservations. Wouldn't some parents think "keys" meant a piano-only class? After I got back from the lake, Lourna and I were at Watershed, waiting for the stage paint to dry. The air smelled of wet paint. The first coat had come out too thin. Patches of wood were exposed in places, like a jigsaw puzzle with half its pieces missing. —I wish we could've named the school after my brother.

—Your *brother*? Lourna looked slightly appalled. She went to the window. I'd opened the windows to help ventilate the barn. —What's he have to do with the school?

—Well, he was a terrific musician.

—Your brother never played an instrument.

—He could play guitar. A little.

—When? In college? I never heard him play.

—Okay, I just miss him. I'm sad he's gone. I wanted to name the school in his honor.

—Naming the school after him won't bring him back, you know.

—That's not the point, Lourna.

She crossed her arms and came towards me. Her hair fell forward, and she touched her temple with one finger like she usually did right before she was going to have a migraine. In worrying about Elizabeth, in always making sure Elizabeth's needs were met, Lourna often

133

forgot to take care of herself. She would skip breakfast, having only a cup of coffee, afraid the food might trigger a migraine, and yet she'd never forget to make Elizabeth her pancakes or her peanut-butter-and-honey sandwich with the crust cut off. It infuriated me how Elizabeth never said thank you unless I prompted her, how she took her mother's devotion for granted.

Sometimes when she ate the meal Lourna had prepared, Elizabeth would turn to the window while she chewed, as if she were in a restaurant, as if a server had brought her the plate. —Elizabeth, tell your mother thank you. She doesn't have to cook for you, you know. Elizabeth would put her hand up to her moving lips, as if to say it's not polite to talk with your mouth full, and sometimes she'd pretend to catch a crumb about to fall out of her mouth. Elizabeth ate in a hurry. She'd drop her plate into the sink and race off to her room, and I'd yell at her to come back, your mother's not your servant. Show some respect.

And how Lourna would follow Elizabeth into the church lobby with a hairbrush and a spray bottle of conditioner. Lourna didn't care about her own appearance, she'd let her hair fall into her face, but her daughter's hair had to be perfect, smooth as a paddle blade. Every Sunday morning, Lourna would brush Elizabeth's hair, fold her collar, kiss her on the forehead, and beam at her beautiful daughter as she rubbed off the smear of lipstick with her thumb. It was practically the only time Elizabeth allowed her mother to touch her, those mornings before Elizabeth did the announcements. And even then, not a word of gratitude.

—What's going on? Lourna said. What happened?

I nudged one of Fred's floor cables with the toe of my shoe.

—Why was the garage door open this morning?

—I have no idea, I said. Maybe I forgot to close it.

—Are you sleeping with someone?

—What? My neck got hot. Yes, I was innocent, but when your wife makes a false accusation, it's hard not to feel burned. —Of course not.

Lourna didn't reply. I thought her silence meant I should keep talking.

—Our marriage is the sacred bond, I said. The foundation of our family. Our household. If I can't manage my *household*, how can I take care of the church?

I'd been married long enough to know you don't want to incorporate church wisdom into an argument with your wife. You shouldn't talk so much. Definitely don't ask her if she's crazy. She's not. The happy-marriage books (I've read them all, folks) say it's better to wait her out and simply "offer your reassuring presence." Put your hand on her shoulder if you think she's ready for your touch. It's a lot of "feeling things out." If you're male, do the opposite of what the voice in your head is telling you. Mine was telling me to figure out what the problem with Lourna was so I could fix it and we could move on and talk about Elizabeth.

—You're not having sex with someone else?

—No, I said. It hurts me you'd need to ask. What does the garage door have to do with anything? Never mind. Listen, Lourna. I think it's time we had a talk.

—So it's true. You are cheating on me.

—No. Sit down, please.

Folks, and I'm still talking to the men: it's never a good idea to tell your wife to sit down. Haven't you watched enough cop shows to realize it's arrogant of you to tell a woman to sit down when there's bad news? As if she can't handle bad news standing up? As if whatever you have to tell her could actually make her faint?

—I'm not gonna sit down. Lourna locked eyes with me. She was no longer massaging the place on her head where the migraines started. Wrongly, I viewed this as a good sign.

—Something happened at the lake, I said. —It's hard to explain.

Lourna kept her back to the window, her hands pressed together in her lap.

—Tell me what you did, Zach. No, wait. Her voice dropped to a whisper. —Not here. Don't confess your crimes in front of our daughter.

—Elizabeth's not here. I'm not confessing anything.

—Elizabeth! Lourna shouted. The window was still open but not by much. —Okay, you're probably right. She can't hear us from Freedom Keys.

—She's not in the music school, I said. She and Nelle took off.

—You see? You tell her to do a simple chore. She never *listens* to you.

—We don't listen to *her*. That's the problem. Do I need to show you?

Lourna and I went next door to Freedom Keys, where the paint fumes were stronger than in the barn. The girls hadn't bothered to open the windows. We found their abandoned brushes, their trays, the paint cans opened. The walls did not have any fresh coat, as I'd expected. I showed Lourna the big "X" Elizabeth had painted on the wall behind the piano.

—I don't want to judge, I said, but I feel like you're deflecting the issue of our daughter's illness, or maybe choosing to ignore it, by manufacturing a bigger crisis.

—So you don't think *adultery* is a crisis?

—I didn't expect you to go to the lake. I know you've had too much sun.

—So you went anyway, with *that woman.*

—If you didn't want me to go, why didn't you tell me?

Lourna went to the desk, reached into the middle drawer, and removed a box of pencils. I wanted to bring up the issue of the paint. I should've cracked open a window. Lourna didn't seem bothered by the smell. She was focused on the pencils. She dumped them out onto the desk. The unsharpened yellow sticks clattered.

—Listen, you don't have to sharpen those, I said. I wanted to show you Elizabeth isn't here. Nelle isn't here. I don't think it's safe for you to be in here, either.

—What're you trying to tell me?

—Elizabeth needs professional help. She thinks Fred…

Lourna picked up a pencil and inserted it into the sharpener and turned the crank. The grinding of the sharpener blade as it shaved wood and graphite into a finer point created a thunderstorm. Was Lourna hoping to trigger a migraine?

—You said Fred wasn't there.

—He wasn't, I'm pretty sure. It was a fisherman. I told you.

—What fisherman? I shouldn't have to tell you I didn't want you to go. You should *know* it would kill me. The four of you, like a family. Like y'all had knocked me off the stage.

—I'm sorry. I invited them before I knew Fred couldn't make it.

—And you went anyway.

—Elizabeth thinks Fred was there. That's a problem.

—I'll bet Rachel didn't tell Fred. Bet she made up the whole rock-symphony excuse. Rachel didn't tell him because she wanted to be with *you.*

—A man pulled Elizabeth out of the water. He thought she was drowning. An innocent mistake. But Elizabeth didn't think so. She freaked out. She nearly clawed him to death. She's cut herself at least twice, and we haven't talked about anything. Not even to each other. Now I'm worried it's too late. She's gone past her limit. Or whatever limits we failed to set for her. Elizabeth won't talk to us. She won't do anything we say.

—Sorry, but I'm still trying to understand how our daughter ended up with a stranger.

—Lourna, I went to the car to get sunscreen. The girls had left the bottle in the car. I thought we'd need more. Rachel was getting lunch started. The girls were swimming. They were having fun. I didn't see the fisherman jump, but Rachel said he'd said he thought a girl was drowning. He jumped into the lake and pulled her out. It happened very fast. The thing is, she thought it was Fred. She attacked the guy. I had to apologize.

—You *weren't* watching her. You probably had your eyes on Rachel.

—I went back for more sunscreen.

—You told me they put sunscreen on in the car.

—Yes, but I know how you hate the sun, and I didn't want to risk bringing home our daughter all burnt to a crisp. I thought a sunburn on our child was the last thing you'd need.

Lourna shoved another pencil into the pencil sharpener.

—Rachel had your attention. Zacharias. I'm *warning* you.

Whatever else Lourna needed to say, she didn't. The pencil had gone into the metal opening at a bad angle, and while Lourna was grabbing it with her hands, trying to reposition the yellow-stick part, her whole body went slack, her legs buckled, and she slumped to the floor. I'd never seen her pass out, but that's what happened.

Lourna passed out from the paint fumes.

STOP LECTURING US AND OPEN YOUR EYES

Nelle, I seriously doubt Lourna fainted from the fumes. We left three cans cracked, not spilled, and the "X" in Mars black on the wall would not have caused her to ~~black~~ lose consciousness. If Zach tries to imply the news of Fred's "grabbing" me caused Lourna to faint, Zach should not have undermined himself when he said, "As if whatever you have to tell her could actually make her faint?" He's either lying or being a hypocrite. Take your pick.

Honestly, if Lourna were the kind of person who fainted at bad news, she'd have fainted when Zach told her about his night in Lester's warehouse with the AK-47. She doesn't faint when he tells her about his abduction, and yet we're supposed to believe she faints after he tells her about "the fisherman" (i.e. Fred)? Lourna's a strong woman. Male narrators usually overlook the strength of female characters, something the end of my story will prove—if he lets me get there. Zach's problem is he's too ~~die~~ didactic. Whether in church or not, he *preaches* too much. Preaching causes blindness. Like staring at the ~~son~~ sun too long.

If he had stopped lecturing and opened his eyes, he'd have *seen* the trauma, the psychological damage, Fred caused me. He'd have *seen* what Lester Hargreve and the Alejandro Brothers were doing to Watershed. He'd have seen what they did backstage.

Backstage, where the ushers stacked the collection plates, Hargreve and his thugs installed a false-bottom casket. A maple casket with an inner lining of puncture-resistant velvet and a hole in the bottom covered with a Velcro-lined velvet flap, which opened onto a hole in the floor leading to a tunneled cave beneath Watershed where the Alejandro Brothers stored more drugs. Nelle, you probably told Fred my story about the hollow at the bottom of the lake. If so, we can assume my story inspired him to instruct the drug dealers to drill a hole through the casket and create a secret chamber beneath Watershed Church.

Not only did he *know* about the drugs, Fred showed the men where to hide them.

Cocaine in the piano and more cocaine under the maple casket. Fred had a vault created behind the "Jesus, Lamb of God" poster and filled the vault with bricks of Saran-Wrapped one-hundred dollar bills. Ben Franklins. I don't know how far the vault went, if it connected with a tunnel or air duct, but they stuffed a lot of Franklins behind the wall. How well did Fred fill the barn with cash and drugs, Nelle? We agree he aided and abetted. Fred.

I'm glad we didn't touch the money or drugs, Nelle. I'm sure you saw enough crime in Houston to know what happens to girls who steal from drug lords. I understand why you would've been too freaked out to tell the cops. Did you talk to Fred before I killed him? Did he tell you what we already know? Did he reveal any of the facts which you, me, Zach, and everybody else listening or not listening to his stupid broadcast can agree on?

Before the vault behind Jesus, before the hollow piano, and before the false-bottom casket, Fred Valenkemp worked late on Saturday nights preparing the stage for Sunday morning services. He was the only one backstage. His presence at Watershed in the nights leading up to the explosion does not strike us as a coincidence. If Fred wasn't working for the Alejandro Brothers, he knew what they were doing. He knew what he was doing when he grabbed me in the lake. In the next chapter, I will correct Zach's record of what happened after the lake. Don't be fooled by his ambiguous pronouns, Nelle. They're simply his way of deflecting responsibility.

I'm glad you're still my friend even though I killed your dad.

PLAUSIBLE DENIABILITY: COVERING HIS YOU KNOW WHAT

Elizabeth never told ~~us~~ me Fred molested her at Salterra Lake. Her sulky mood and her odd behavior at dinner (crumpling up a plastic grocery bag while ~~we~~ Lourna and I were enjoying our meal?) led me to believe something bad had happened to ~~us~~ her.

~~She was~~ We were *all* too afraid to talk about the lake.

Lourna and I took Elizabeth to a psychiatrist. The psychiatrist recommended a book on "how to talk to your teenage daughter." We were too late. The book said spend more time with your daughter. I took Elizabeth to a biker's convention on Main. We looked for my brother's Harley. No one owned the model. The same book said give your daughter compliments. I said you're beautiful. I love you. Ask her questions without sounding like you're spying.

I wanted to ask if she had a boyfriend. Lourna said we shouldn't.

A boyfriend. ~~Funny.~~ Not funny. Way off the mark.

Here's what we learned: her favorite book is *Night* by Elie Wiesel. Her favorite movies ~~are~~ were musicals: *West Side Story*, *My Fair Lady*, *The King and I*, anything by Rodgers and Hammerstein. Her favorite place was the Guess store at North Star Mall in San Antonio. Her favorite color was and is black. Her favorite animal is Shadow. Her favorite singer is Kurt Cobain. Her favorite band is Nirvana. Her favorite food? Pizza. What else?

I asked Jesus to help me figure out what was going on in my daughter's mind. Why was she so quiet? Why did she stay in her room all afternoon? Why did she no longer take showers or bathe? My mentor at New Foundations baptized her when she was a baby, so the deterioration of her personal hygiene didn't concern me as much as you'd expect. Like the cutting. ~~We assumed it was a phase.~~ I complimented her on her new way of keeping herself smelling nice and fresh. I said it was clever and resourceful not to waste water. ~~We didn't know.~~

Plus, the next few months treated the Hembreys well. No break-ins, no trespassers, no more of Lester's men barging into my house in the middle of the night to abduct me. I preached the Word, and as Lester promised, Watershed was starting to prosper.

Lourna increased the quantity and quality of our weekly newsletters. She put "From the Desk of Pastor Zacharias P. Hembrey" in the upper-right-hand corner. The first two paragraphs were always positive: "I believe 1994 will be an amazing year for you, your family, and you'll achieve greatness in every aspect of your life! I want to thank you for faithfully serving Watershed Church." For the third paragraph, Lourna would type what we were asking for in bold: "**I am asking all those who serve at Watershed Church to attend our Mandatory Leadership Seminar this Saturday at Watershed from 9AM to 3PM**. Lunch provided."

For the folks who only glanced at these newsletters, who only heard "thanks" and maybe saw the words in bold but didn't actually read them, who glanced a second time, and who before long skimmed back and forth over the bold letters in the middle of the page, thinking what's that all about—for these folks, the "**I am asking all**" became a wonderful wormhole. Less than a third who read the letter would actually show up. Everybody found it a Big Inconvenience. Still, nobody could stop hearing the "**I am asking all**."

Like the voice of God. Brilliant job, Lourna.

Our congregants flocked from San Antonio and the surrounding towns east and west of the interstate. Men wore casual suits with bolo ties and women sported loose cotton dresses or Mexican dresses with cowboy boots or high heels. They flocked in station wagons and sedans. They carpooled. They rode the bus. We added an evening service. We had outdoor barbecues. More horse-trough baptisms. We bought more instruments for Freedom Keys, enrolled more children. We gave our musicians a raise. Before the sound check, before any of us got to touch our instruments, my Brother Fred controlled every aspect of the stage's setup. Our congregants loved the amazing effects he created on his synthesizers during the service. I didn't see any evidence of what Rachel had warned me about, his possessiveness. Despite what my daughter writes to Nelle about the threats he made in the dungeon, Fred never said anything to me about not talking to Rachel again. Neither Fred nor Elizabeth ever told me about their conversation in the studio. Elizabeth never told me he'd threatened to blow up the church.

I still don't understand her purpose behind the grocery bag on the dinner table.

A magic trick?

HOW TO GET YOUR PARENTS TO STOP TALKING

Wad a plastic grocery bag in your fist as tightly as you can. Release it on the dinner table and put your ear close by and act like you *seriously* need to hear the crackling.

THE SHERIFF ALREADY LIVES IN TOWN

One day Rachel and I were in the parking lot behind Daylight Donuts. I had a lot of drugs on my person, but it's not like y'all think. I'd shown Rachel an Rx for Lourna's migraines. Rachel said those pills were okay, but did I want to try some others? Turned out she'd amassed a small pharmacy inside her trunk. Hundreds of samples she'd peddle to physicians in different hospitals across the county. All legal as part of her job as a drug rep.

—We switched Fred's medication, she said, after she handed me the drug samples. We'd had coffee at Daylight, and I thought I we were saying goodbye. Caffeine makes Rachel chatty. She had more things to say about her husband. —He wasn't responding well to the old sedatives. These drugs. That's the thing. You can't be afraid to try the new ones.

I heard a car pull in behind us and turned. It was Sheriff Lufkin. He parked and heaved himself out of the driver's seat. —Morning, y'all. Glad I bumped into you, pastor.

Normally in this part of the service, I would preach how people don't simply "bump" into each other. God has a plan for every one of us. Jesus spat on the ground and put clay on a blind man's eyes and told him to wash off the clay in the pool of Siloam. Y'all think the blind man knew *ahead of time* the works of God would be revealed in him?

I don't think so.

Sheriff Lufkin was a large Southern Missouri man who came from a family of watermelon farmers up near Kennett, Missouri. You could hear the boot-heel in his accent. I don't know how he wound up in Texas. At the time, I didn't want to know. After my meeting with Lester Hargreve, I didn't want Lufkin anywhere near Watershed.

Today, I'd welcome him. I'd welcome him as a Brother-in-Christ. Unfortunately, he attends First Baptist.

His duty belt held a panoply of intimidation. Silver handcuffs, walkie-talkie, baton, pepper spray, heavy keys, flashlight, gloves, and of course his Smith & Wesson 9 mm.

—The morning *is* glorious, I said. What can we do for you?

—Drove by your church last night. We got a noise complaint. The lights were on.

Rachel slammed the lid of her trunk, and the *thunk* made me flinch. At Daylight, she'd told me how she gets doctors to buy her products: First make him think you're his friend. Find out what brand of wine, whiskey, or cigar he likes (it's always a man, always wine, whiskey, or cigars). You give him the special gift and along with your pitch you sneak in the expectation of a future event: —So, Dr. Sheppard, you'll use Despartole for the next ten patients who complain of persistent daily headaches? Wonderful, and don't forget we're having lunch next week at Rebelle. I can't wait to meet your wife and kids.

Although I couldn't say I approved of her tactics, I knew I had a lot to learn from Rachel Valenkemp. She was already serving as Leader of Youth Ministries, but I believed she could take over some of Lourna's responsibilities as financial manager.

—That's not unusual, Rachel said to Sheriff Lufkin. —My husband works at night.

—Ma'am, I don't mean to be rude, but I was talking to Pastor Zacharias.

—You got a problem with a woman offering an explanation?

—If you'll let me talk to Zacharias about the lights, I'll let you get back to your day.

Sheriff Lufkin's lip quivered beneath his moustache. He hiked up his duty belt. Why didn't I simply defuse their hostility by introducing the sheriff to Rachel?

His Smith & Wesson. I hadn't seen a gun since my night in the warehouse. While my eyes locked onto his sidearm and wouldn't let go, I couldn't speak. It took a lot of willpower for me to stay calm and keep my head from turning into a lava lamp. What did the sheriff see at Watershed? What did Fred see? Coils of worry crawled into my shoulders.

—What she means, sheriff, is that her husband works at the church at night. He's my keyboardist. Great guy. He makes amazing music. I'll tell him to keep it down.

Sheriff Lufkin reached for his pen and notepad. —Ma'am, what's your husband's name?

—You're asking me? I thought you wanted to talk to Zacharias.

—His name is Fred Valenkemp, I said. The Valenkemps live on the corner of Franklin and Main down the road from the church. Rachel scowled at me, and I could've kicked myself. Why was I giving the sheriff so much free information? The prescription bag loaded with Rachel's samples almost slipped out of my hands. I rolled it tightly with my fingers.

—Thanks for letting us know, sheriff. I'm sure it was Fred. He's setting up a new lighting system. God bless him. Probably had the PA too loud. I'll tell him to keep it down.

—Watershed's bringing all kinds of folks to Salterra.

—We welcome everyone, yes.

—Now we got Lester Hargreve, the sheriff said. Opening a tavern?

—It's called Inferno, sheriff. I haven't been there.

—Just what this town needs, the sheriff said. Another bar for the drunks. Guess you can't have one without the other. Bars to turn them out. Churches to receive them.

—To receive the blessings of our Lord. Yes, sir.

Rachel folded her arms across her chest and turned to the sheriff. —You have anything better to do than drive around at night staring into people's windows like a peeping Tom?

Sheriff Lufkin licked his teeth again. His upper lip rolled beneath the woolly bear of his moustache. He looked like he needed a toothpick.

—Ma'am, I don't like your attitude. I saw the lights on. There was a noise complaint. I'm following up with Pastor Zacharias. I'm doing my job.

—Great. I'll do mine.

—So you understand. The pastor and I work with the same class of people.

—What sort of people are you referring to? Rachel said.

—Listen, sheriff. She doesn't mean to be rude.

—Lowlifes. The sheriff hiked up his duty belt. —Pastor and I spend a lot of time listening to lowlifes and their problems. I'll need to speak with your husband. Sheriff Lufkin glanced at his notepad. —Mr. Fred Valenkemp. I'll need to know *his* problem.

—My husband's low, but not like them. He's not feeling well.

—If he's sick, why's he working nights?

—He's a musician. The work is therapeutic.

Sheriff Lufkin turned to me with a look of mild frustration that disappeared only when he waved to the local barber who'd come out with a box of glazed donuts.

—When he's feeling better, I told the sheriff, I'll put you in touch with Fred.

—Thank you. Y'all have a good rest of your day.

BUT AS WE NOW KNOW FROM THE FACTS

Zach never put the sheriff in touch with Fred. The sheriff never did his *job* by questioning Fred Valenkemp. That the sheriff never followed up on such an obvious lead should tell you about Salterra's law enforcement or lack thereof. It's crappy. The system needs an overhaul.

Thursday, I waited for Zach to leave for rehearsal before I snuck out of the house. Normally once a month, the band goes over new tunes at Watershed. Once a month for an hour or so, until Fred says the tunes are good enough to perform for Sunday service. Normally they rehearse Saturday nights, but this was the Saturday of the stupid Lock-in, where they herd everybody into the barn to play games and watch Jesus movies overnight, or whatever.

After checking in on Lourna, zonked out after taking Rachel's new drugs, I grabbed my friend from the bathroom, took a pair of scissors from my own room, and three steak knives from the kitchen. I wrapped the knives with a couple of church newsletters, and I placed the knives and the scissors with my friend into my Trapper Keeper. I biked to the Valenkemps.

We're not far.

I found you in the backyard whacking the trunk of your magnolia tree with a red Wiffleball bat. The dented plastic made a hollow pinging sound when it struck the tree. Behind the oaks on the horizon above your house, the Texas sun rolled like a detached head. I lowered my Trapper Keeper of sharp objects and approached you slowly.

—Where's your mom?

I figured Rachel was already at the church, but I wanted to make sure.

—Church, you said. They're all there. Now she sings in the band, you know. My dad didn't want her out of his sight. They were fighting.

—Think she'll come home early?

—Not until rehearsal's over.

—Good. I unzipped my Trapper Keeper and showed you the tools. I took out the razor.

—What's that?

I unfolded the blade, tightened my grip around the handle, and sliced your cheek. You stumbled backwards as the blood dripped down your face. It took a moment for you to realize what I'd done.

—It's gonna sting a little, I said. It'll heal. It'll heal soon enough. You see the bone on the handle? These animals lose them every year, but they grow back.

—What the hell, Liz?

—Easy, easy. (I didn't think of what Fred said to me in the lake until much later. I wanted to tell you not to call me "Liz" or "Elizabeth" anymore, but hadn't yet come up with another name. I didn't want anything Biblical. Later, I would settle for "Elena.")

While you held your wounded cheek, I explained:

—It's so you won't be blamed for what we're about to do. This way you can tell your dad you tried to stop me. We fought, and you tried to stop me, okay? Your turn.

—What?

I pointed to where I wanted you to cut me.

You held the razor up to my face but couldn't do it, your hand shook too much, and I think you started to cry. I grabbed your hand with the razor and pressed the blade into my cheek and dragged it sideways. Relief flowed through me before I felt the blood. Tears came to my eyes and fell and mixed with my blood.

You were in shock. I smeared my blood across my face, and yours across your face, and at some point we realized we needed to break the spell of seriousness, so I tickled you under the arms and we laughed like the priests of Baal and it was our custom to cut ourselves with knives and cry aloud until the blood gushed out of us.

Or like when boys kill their first deer, Nelle. —You have the key?

You kicked the red Wiffleball bat into the grass. The key was in your pocket and you took it out and we went to the dungeon and you inserted the key into the lock.

—We're not gonna do too much, you said. Are we?

I handed you two steak knives. I wadded up the newsletters, covered in my blood, and dropped them onto the carpet. First I went to the liquor cabinet. I opened the schnapps bottle, put some liquor on Fred's microfiber cloths and wiped my cheek with it. I wiped your cheek. The rest of the liquor I poured over the mixing board. It wasn't plugged in. No smoke or sparks. The schnapps flowed around the knobs and beneath the volume sliders. A waterfall.

—Go ahead, I said, pointing to the speakers. —Cut them.

—Seriously? We could get in so much trouble.

—You won't, I said. Only *I* will. Remember?

With a steak knife in each hand you stabbed the stereo speakers multiple times and hollered with joy. You enjoyed the stabbing, Nelle. Don't lie. You threw a steak knife at a painting on the wall, *The Valley from Montserrat* by Jose Vives-Atsara, and with the second knife you sliced through the grill cloth of another speaker. Fred had surge protectors but he'd unplugged them. (I guess he didn't trust the protectors.) We were the storm. You plunged your steak knife into the cone of the subwoofer.

—Right on the money, I said.

I threw the empty schnapps bottle at the computer. The bottle left a web of cracks in the monitor screen. I took a microphone stand and slammed the round metal base onto the keyboard. Some of the keys popped off, and the board split in half. With the scissors, I snipped all the cables that fed into the synthesizers and I cut the wires off the silver headphones and smashed the headphones with the microphone stand. We tore out pages of sheet music, grabbed music books off the shelves, and tipped the bookshelf onto the carpet.

You carved something into the surface of the desk.

—Not there, I said. Only this side. Let's get the equipment.

You obeyed, and I wondered, Had I killed us? Would *Fred* follow through?

Last, we did the synthesizers. Two keyboards were missing from the rack. I assumed Fred took those to rehearsal, but the others were still mounted. The Fender Rhodes lay in its suitcase beneath the card table. From the side, the case looked like a child's coffin. I opened it up but I couldn't get the keyboard out, so I smeared my blood across the keys.

—*Freedom*, I said. Now if only we had some music.

You turned on one of the synthesizers and pressed the "demo" button and out came Scott Joplin's "The Entertainer." —Good enough, I said. We left the demo playing while we broke the other synthesizers, ripping them off their stands and smashing them against one another, a beautiful collision of plastic buttons and keys and knobs and dials.

By the time we finished with the dungeon, our sweaty clothes clung to our bodies.

—Think that's enough? you said.

I rubbed your cheek. The blood had dried on your face. —Enough, I said. I pressed my thumb against your razor cut. —*This* would've been enough.

THAT OTHER TIME FRED ALMOST BAILED

I usually try to walk in the mornings when I'm working on my sermons. One time I got stuck in a passage, and I went from the church to the Valenkemps. Rachel sat at the kitchen table, and I tapped on the screen door. I made a comment about the weather, and somehow we got to talking about cleaning. She'd helped me sweep the floors of Watershed Church shortly after Fred was hired, and I guess I wanted to return the favor.

After we had some coffee, I went to the sink and grabbed a dirty plate, rinsed it, and stacked it on the counter above the dish washer. I cleaned a few other plates and flipped her hand towel over my shoulder. I didn't turn around until I'd cleaned everything in the sink.

While I scrubbed the plates, I heard Rachel behind me, pacing. She'd quit objecting to my cleaning after she saw the bartender towel-flip. When I was done, she came up behind me and put a serrated knife onto the pile of wet cutlery. Her hand grazed the back of my wrist. I stepped away from the sink, and she noticed my shirt. The lower half of my shirt and the waistline of my pants were soaked with water.

She laughed at the wet mess of my clothes. —I'll get you a dry shirt.

I wanted to tell her it wasn't necessary but she'd already left the kitchen. Family photos were pinned to the door of her fridge with bottlecap magnets. Most of them of Nelle. Nelle as a little girl outside the Astrodome. Nelle at a picnic, wrapped in a mermaid-themed tablecloth. Nelle and Rachel at Disneyland, posing with Mickey Mouse and Cinderella.

The only photo of Fred I could find was of the musician seated on some bleachers, like at a football stadium, only these were empty, and Fred was eating from what looked like a box of popcorn. In the photo he holds his hand up, palm facing the camera, and the gesture makes him slightly out of focus. It's clear by the raised hand he doesn't want his picture taken. He appears to be smiling but his eyes are startled, even angry.

—This is all I could find, Rachel said. It should fit you.

Her voice pulled me from the world of the photo. —That's all right. I'll walk around. I'll dry out in no time. The T-shirt remained against her stomach. —Thanks, though.

In the viburnum outside, the birds were making a ruckus.

—I can tell you why Fred left town. He had a recording opportunity.

—Really? (I tried not to sound bothered. It would be a big deal if Fred didn't show for service the next day and we had to perform without him.) —Know when he'll return?

—Later tonight, I hope.

—Me, too. I cleared my throat. Folks, this was the closest I ever came to telling her about Hargreve and what his thugs might be doing at night, what our church might be holding. This would have been Rachel's best chance to tell *me* about Fred's homicidal tendencies, but in all fairness I don't think she knew he'd be capable of murder, much less of Committing a Terrorist Act in the name of petty retaliation.

—Before I stopped by, I said, I was working on my sermon. I like to plan it out in my head while I'm walking. Know what the Biblical Hebrew word for "field" is?

—No. She turned to me, and my throat tightened. If she wanted to tell me she knew of *another* reason Fred left town, a legitimate reason, she never did.

—It's *sadeh*, I said. *Sadeh*, field.

Fred did show up for service that time. If he hadn't, Lester would have killed me. I'm sure of it. I don't know why Fred was late. Maybe he'd already decided to bomb the church, and he had second thoughts about showing up. Showing up two nights before, surrounded by his band, he could have changed his mind. Then maybe he worried his absence would cause suspicion. What goes through the mind of a church bomber?

—If he doesn't make it tonight, I told Rachel. I'll have to find another keyboardist for Sunday. I can't have my Brothers not showing for rehearsals. It looks bad.

—I'm sorry, Rachel said. Fred didn't tell me anything. He'll be here.

—Can I ask you a question?

—Shoot.

—You think my stage has enough black?

—Sure. Where's Elizabeth?

—At home. Why?

—They're getting close. Nelle wanted her to come over this weekend.

—We got the Lock-in Saturday night. It's gonna be busy.

—I'll tell her we'll wait and see.

THEY ASK HIM FOR A SHAVE

I was admitted on Friday, the day after I trashed Fred's studio. Since then, I've learned a few things: The older women of Warm Springs aren't ashamed to ask the male nurse for a shave. In fact, they'll shout loud and clear for him to shave the hairs off their upper lips and chins. —*Come on, Lafey, I need a shave! Let me do it!* "Lafey," short for Lafayette—he told me—a family name the first-born male has inherited going on four generations. A ranching family with fifty acres outside Driftwood. The women shame Lafey for not letting them shave themselves. Women who are crazy. Wanting unsupervised access to a razor. Are you kidding me?

IF YOUR RIGHT EYE CAUSES YOU TO SIN

—Did Nelle really ask her to come over? I said to Rachel. You don't have to force Nelle to be friends with Elizabeth, if that's what you're doing.

—I'm not.

—Good. Because we're getting Elizabeth professional help.

—Good.

When we went to Rachel's house in search of Fred, I noticed their living quarters for the first time: the worn Persian rug, the scuffed breakfast-nook table, the bookshelves loaded with leather-bound classics, framed portraits on the walls. This wasn't the home of an itinerant family as I'd imagined. This place didn't square with my image of the man in the black suit with his suitcases, the one who'd auditioned for us in the barn. The house displayed the messy permanence of a real family who'd chosen to settle down. The house had been *lived in*.

Rachel and I descended into Fred's studio. The order and tidiness of the room reminded me of his fastidiousness and of how carefully he always prepared the stage at church. Rolls of gaff and electrical tape lay in neat rows on a card table. Color-coded labels marked the volume dials of his soundboards. Two pairs of leather shoes and a pair of slippers were lined up on a square of carpet behind the door. The thermostat was set to sixty-eight degrees, and on the floor, plugged into the wall, a humidifier puffed wisps of steam.

The studio wasn't the man cave I'd pictured, but a well-organized sound laboratory, the studio of a professional musician. So Fred has landed another gig, I thought, and he's too busy to show up for our rehearsal. Well, we were lucky to have him. He's on to bigger and better things.

Rachel was distraught. She took a few laps around the studio, sunk down onto one of the chairs, and raised her arm as if to shield her eyes from the sun. —He's not here, she said.

—He'll turn up, I said. I should get back to Watershed. Maybe he's already there.

—I'll wait here. I'll call you if he shows up.

Her eyelids dropped, lifted.

—Hey, I asked her. What's the matter? You okay?

I can't tell y'all the color of her eyes. No personally identifiable information allowed on the air. However, I will say her irises had little flecks of rust in them, or whatever mineral the dark pebbles mix with at the bottom of a clear riverbed.

—Your eyes, I said.

—What?

—Nothing. It's just, back in the day, when we partook—

(Partake. Partook. Partaken?)

—Lourna's eyes would do the same thing. What yours are doing now.

—What're they doing?

WE INTERRUPT THIS RADIO BROADCAST TO BRING YOU

Fresh-Lease On-the-Go™ gets rid of those bad, lingering odors. Perfect for sofas, bedding, carpets, closets, pet barns, dog crates, clothing, ~~and Fred Valenkemp~~. Fresh-Lease On-the-Go™ is safe around dogs and cats. NOT for use around birds, bats, lizards, sea turtles, and snakes, unless you're talking about the ancient serpent, the Devil dragon, then fire away.

Fresh-Lease On-the-Go™ comes in a convenient 2.8 ml travel-size bottle, so you can take it wherever you go. Simply spray material with Fresh-Lease On-the-Go™ until slightly damp, and you will witness *amazing* results. Fresh-Lease On-the-Go™ is safe on virtually all Christian fabrics, including burlap and wool. Not for use on leather, suede, or silk.

Fresh-Lease On-the-Go™ contains water, alcohol, ~~mysterious toxic~~ odor eliminator, and natural fragrances.

Caution: Use only as directed. Intentional misuse by deliberately concentrating and ~~slashing~~ inhaling the contents can be harmful or fatal. Help stop inhalation abuse. For more information, please write to ~~Pastor Zacharias P. Hembrey; Watershed Project Church; 465 Franklin Road; Salterra, TX 78666~~. (Nice try, Liz.) Some hard surfaces may become damp and slippery when sprayed. Avoid accidents such as falls.

Do not spray Fresh-Lease On-the-Go™ directly into your face. If eye contact occurs, rinse well with cold water. Keep out of reach of children and small pets. Fresh-Lease On-the-Go™ may be harmful if swallowed. In case of ingestion, seek medical attention immediately.

Available at your local grocery store or pharmacy. Enjoy a fresh new lease on life as you spray Fresh-Lease On-the-Go™ on any material and enjoy a pleasant, worry-free day!

DON'T GET HUNG UP ON THE WALL

When I got back to the church Thursday night, Lester Hargreve was waiting for me. Things could get ugly with Lester around, so I tried to dismiss the band. I told them to go home.

—No rehearsal tonight, folks. Something's come up.

—What're you talking about? my drummer said. The rest of the band gathered behind him, like they were a posse and they'd nominated him as their spokesperson. We came all this way, my drummer said. We lugged all our equipment in here. We're not leaving.

Had they spoken to Lester Hargreve? Could they tell he was in charge?

In my office, Lester paced back and forth behind my desk. On stage the bassist was setting up the PA, uncoiling power cords, a task Fred normally did. Perhaps they were relieved Fred hadn't shown up. They could set up the stage however they wanted. They could rehearse without his overbearing presence. Prove to me the show would go on without him.

—Guys, we'll do a run-though an hour before service, I promise.

My guys stomped across the stage, ignoring me. They plugged in their microphones, noodled on their guitars. Did they only listen to me when Fred was around? If they defied me in rehearsal, they might defy me during the service, or in the middle of a performance. A church whose followers disrespect their pastor doesn't stand a chance. But with Lester in the office, I had bigger problems than a group of mutinous musicians.

Lester wouldn't stay quiet much longer. He wanted a consultation. He kept signaling for me to step into my office. I swallowed a lump in my throat. I felt an ache in my teeth.

He stood behind my desk in a pair of jeans and a beige trench coat. He'd shaved. All that remained of his pirate's beard was a soul patch that protruded from the middle of his chin. He must have shaved in the dark, as I sometimes did, because he had nicks all over his face and on the tips of his earlobes, which still sported the gold hoops. His do-rag was tucked under a beaver-tail cowboy hat. He looked tired and agitated. He'd traded freedom for servitude. Traded a beach-bum life for a life of street crime. He lived under the pressure of the Alejandro Brothers now. The bags under his eyes were like a pair of nickels dipped in purple ink.

—We've got a problem, he said. Sit down.

—If it's all right with you, I'll stand.

I closed the door to my office. I shut the blinds.

—What's the problem, Lester?

—Some of our product has disappeared. It's on you to recover it.

—Well, I wouldn't know. I don't have anything to do with your product.

—It was lost under your watch, so it's on you. And you'll have to pay without raising suspicion at the bank. The sheriff's getting curious. He's been driving by at night.

Lester leaned back on his heels, and I thought I heard a squelching sound, as if his boots were full of water. —I'd hate for there to be an accident, with all these people inside.

—There doesn't need to be an accident. I'm cooperating. I'm giving them access to the church. What happens at night is their business.

—It's your business, too. You haven't told anyone about our project?

—No, Lester. I swear to God.

—Does it count more when a man of God swears? Or does it count less?

Lester opened his trench coat to show me a Browning Hi-Power holstered to his side. The butt of the 9mm pistol, black and oily, sagged under his arm. His damp grimy T-shirt clung to his skin. He closed his coat and glanced over my shoulder. —What about him?

I could smell Fred before I could see him. That lunchbox stink, the odor of cold cuts trapped in a solid metal container for days without ventilation.

Fred in his black suit, with the open quotation mark of his little eyebrow bandage, asking what he'd walked into. The case for his Fender Rhodes clicked against the floor when he set it down, the tap of hard plastic against the wood floor like the tap-release of a trigger safety. The rest of the band remained outside warming up. The opening bars of "Jesus I'll Never Forget" crashed through the window panes, and the bass notes buzzed in my tailbone.

Why won't they just go home? I thought.

—Fred's our keys man, I said. He doesn't know anything.

Lester's eyes flicked sideways between the two of us. His long fillet knife came out and did a little dance in the air: *eenie, meenie, miney mo.* Fred wiped his nose. I closed the door and locked it. Feeling a rush of martyrdom, I put myself between Fred and Lester, just to let Lester know he couldn't attack my Brother without slicing through me first.

—I know you, Fred said to Lester. Where have I seen you before?

—Hargreve owns Inferno, I said. The new bar in town.

—No, I know him from somewhere else. I'm not sure where.

Lester remained quiet. He smelled worse than Fred, like catfish. I almost expected flies to swarm these two men. Lester's nails were dirty. I pictured him curled up with the gun on a soiled mattress, or in a sleeping bag beneath his bar. He'd picked up a donation card off my desk and was reading it. —Wyatt Hasselbach prays for the happy arrival of his baby girl, Layla. May she receive all of God's blessings. Amen. Then Lester laughed and flicked the card away.

The card knifed through the air and fell beneath my desk.

—If you can't replace the missing product, Lester said, and I know you can't, then you owe us seven thousand dollars. Seven thousand for what's missing.

—All right, I said. I'll get you seven thousand.

—Except the money's been missing for two weeks. Two weeks too long. So there's interest to pay. Seven thousand plus interest comes to twelve thousand. You bring twelve thousand in cash to Inferno. Has to be cash. And you cannot attract attention. You have twenty-four hours. If it's not there by this time tomorrow, you're a dead man. Him, too.

—I can get you the money, I said, knowing I'd have no way of getting this money any time soon, much less within twenty-four hours. —I'm no Judas, though. I've been doing this the way y'all wanted. I'm cooperating, minding my own business, growing my church.

Behind me, Fred shifted on his feet. —Tell your boss to go fuck himself.

—What'd he just say? Lester rubbed his saucer eyes.

—Nothing, I said. Fred talks to himself.

—I said tell your boss to go fuck himself, Fred said. We're not paying.

—Wait. I felt my throat constrict, my stomach dropping into my knees. —Fred's had a long day. He doesn't know anything. Fred, let me handle this, okay? We'll comply.

One of our female vocalists had begun singing. Behind the door, verses rang loud and out of tune: *"Jesus, I'll never forget, what you've done for me..."* Without Fred to mark off the time, they were butchering the song. Rushed, flat, definitely too loud.

I was about to scream when Fred rushed past the desk and popped Lester in the throat, a direct jab to the man's voice box. Lester's eyes went wide, his mouth turned into a silent oval, and as he winced he stumbled backwards. Struggling for breath, he reached for his gun, but Fred was on him. Fred ripped the Browning Hi-Power out of its holster, threw it towards me. I kicked it across the floor. The gun slid between the goal posts of my two potted ivy plants.

What happened next happened with all the stark hallucinatory feel of a slow-motion Moses Parting the Red Sea: Fred took the fillet knife from Lester and stabbed him through the gumball cyst, pinning him to the wall. The Red Sea of Lester's Blood shot in two directions. One spurt hit his cheek and the other cascaded down his arm. The laceration of the cyst released the most foul stench of sulfur and sauerkraut. My knees turned to gazelle knees again, and I looked away. A hot ball of vomit soured my throat. Above the sound of the band gunning through "Jesus Medley," above Lester's screams, I heard a jingle:

Don't get hung up on the wall.
Not at all, no, not at all.
Treat yourself to a delicious Pall Mall!

When had I written this one? The fillet knife had pierced Lester's arm. His fingers twitched. His screams tore through the jingle in my ears and through the band's noise, and Lester pawed weakly at Fred with his free hand. Fred clutched Lester by the throat, dug his fingers into his gullet. Lester's eyes bulged. Blood poured down his arm and spattered the floor.

I grabbed Fred by the shoulders, trying to throw him off Lester, but Fred was strong and he didn't let up. He would strangle Lester. He'd kill him in my office. I reached between the ivy and picked up the gun, not intending to use it, I was terrified, but I wanted to show them I had it, I was in control. I held the grip and kept my index finger away from the trigger. The gun weighed in my hand. A tension settled in the muscles of my forearm.

—Fred, I yelled. Let him go! You're choking him.

Fred kept his gaze on Lester. He knew exactly what he was doing. He had no intention of letting go. The calculated nature of his movements, the fact that he'd wasted no effort pinning Lester against the wall, stabbing him through the wrist, showed a side of him I'd never seen.

His fingers digging deeper into Lester's throat bespoke of an urgent need, a desire to erase, to extinguish, to kill. The knees bent, the hands locked, the eyes staring, Fred willing death forward, walking death over the line. He'd become less a man of faith and more like Lester and his crowd, someone capable of murder. Lester would die of blood loss, or he'd suffocate, and if these were the two outcomes, neither was enough for Fred. Neither would satisfy him.

I raised the barrel. Slid my finger through the trigger guard.

—Come on, folks. Let's all calm down. We can sort this out. My voice wobbled. The barrel pointed down at Lester's hat, which had fallen in the scuffle behind the desk. I couldn't keep my hand steady. The idea of shooting someone was revolting, ungodly. The gun shook in my hand. Behind me, on stage, the church music surged:

Would you be free from the burden of sin?
There's power in the blood, power in the blood.
Would you o'er evil a victory win?
There's wonderful power in the blood.

Somehow the gun went off, the report rang in my ears, and the sting of cordite drifted through the office. I'd blown a hole in my desk the size of a cantaloupe.

Both men turned towards me, stunned. Lester's eyes darted from me to Fred. I dropped the gun and kicked it back between the plants. Lester peeled Fred's hands off his throat, freed himself. The band stopped playing. The whole barn had gone absolutely still.

Lester's blood spread over the floor like some crucifixion reenactment. Lester screamed as he struggled to pull the knife out of his arm.

With his legs crumpled beneath him, the blade began to tear at the wound. His face paled. His eyes roamed in their sockets. Dark blood soaked the sleeve of his trench coat. I grabbed the knife with both hands, closed my eyes, and ripped it out of the wall. As the blade slid uncleanly from Lester's flesh, I heard bones cracking. Like pulling a steak knife out of a T-bone. Lester whimpered. He cradled his bloody arm and ran from the office. I thought of chasing him down, wondering what he'd tell the Alejandro Brothers, what they'd do to us if they saw his wrist, if they learned what my keyboardist had done, but I knew I wouldn't catch him. Besides, I had Fred to deal with, Fred, who was staring down at his own hands, covered in Lester's blood.

—Nearly broke my fingers. Fred wiped his hands on his pants. Where's the gun? We still have his gun, don't we? Let's go after him. Finish him off.

—No, I said. Why'd you do that? Why'd you stab him?

—Some wounds must be lanced. His voice drifted a moment as he struggled to refocus. Not a nice man. My wife is nice. People take advantage. Sometimes a good lancing eases the pressure. Razor would've done it better, but you use what you have. Speaking of razors, we need to talk about your daughter.

—Elizabeth doesn't know Lester. She doesn't know anything about this. Now I need to figure out what to do. The Alejandro Brothers are going to want their money. I'll have to go to the bank. Take out a loan. These guys don't mess around, Fred. They're in a cartel.

—I'll take care of it.

—No, Fred. I don't want you involved. I'll figure this out.

—I'm already involved.

The door to the office swung open, and Martha, our lead vocalist, burst into the room holding my cup of chamomile tea. The paper tab of the tea bag (Martha knows very well, I always take a minimum of *two* bags, helps soothe the throat, but I wasn't going to fuss at her for the oversight, we had a lot going on)—the paper tab of chamomile swung from the lid of my special Jesus thermos. —Y'all okay? Martha said. Oh, Lord. That's a lot of blood.

—Thanks, Martha. I took the tea. We're fine. Be right there.

I shoved her out and shut the door. I didn't know what to say. If I didn't get the Alejandro Brothers their money, I'd have to cancel the Lock-in. No question. I'd have to cancel the service, shut down the church, head back to San Antonio. I couldn't return to New Foundations. I'd have to find another House of Worship. My preaching days were coming to an end, it seemed. I was prepared to make an announcement to this effect when something Fred had said shuttled back to me, his words resounding like a bell or a trumpet you hear above the fray, a clear voice above the river of chords supporting your two-part melody.

—You said you're *already involved*. What did you mean?

—Nothing. Rachel saw him. At the lake. When y'all were together.

It hit me: The fisherman was Lester. Lester was the man who'd grabbed my daughter. I felt my shoulders drop. I tugged on my shirt collar. It made sense. The pieces clicked into place. In her panic, Elizabeth had thought it was Fred, but it was actually Lester. Lester had wanted to send a message that afternoon, that he could get to me.

That question he'd asked me at the warehouse: *Wonder why those men didn't go after your family?*

They didn't go after my family because he'd kept them away, and now he was saying he couldn't keep them away, any of them, so he'd go after my family himself.

He'd grabbed Elizabeth. Snatched her out of the lake. He could have killed her, drowned her on the spot. He *could* kill her, and there was nothing I could do about it. That day, I hadn't recognized him when we'd crossed paths in the field. The harsh sun. Too focused on the stupid sunscreen. Of course, his beard was gone and the sleeve of his trench coat would have covered up the cyst. It's amazing what we miss when we're distracted.

I'd waved to this man. He waved to me. I'd looked right past him. He looked right past me. He'd gotten close enough. He'd caused my daughter to fly into a rage. Now the Alejandro Brothers were pressuring him to collect money from us. Had he stolen from them?

—Can we talk about Elizabeth? Fred lifted his Fender Rhodes off the floor.

I studied the disaster of my office. Pages across the floor. Blood on the wall and on the donation cards. Chairs overturned. My wooden cross off kilter, my desk shot through, and of course the hole where the fillet knife sank like a dart through Lester's arm. The gun between the potted ivy. Elizabeth would've been shocked to see my office in such a disarray. She's so polite and docile. The sight of a mess in anyone's workplace would have upset her terribly.

—Go home, Fred. I'll clean this up. I got to figure out how to get their money.

—Make sure everybody comes to the Lock-in.

—We can't worship here anymore. It's not safe.

—Don't cancel anything. God is watching us. We have the Lock-in, and the service. Everyone's counting on us. It's going to be perfect. After the service, you can do anything you want, but the Lock-in must happen. Understand?

Fred's threatening tone only confirmed in my mind that his attack on Lester hadn't been entirely spontaneous or out of character. I wondered why he was so adamant. It's possible Fred had stolen the drugs himself. If they assumed Lester had stolen from them, the Alejandro Brothers would bump him off, and Fred could step in and take Lester's place. Or maybe the Alejandro Brothers had approached Fred after he'd heard them at night. Maybe they'd already poached my keyboardist. Fred's involvement wasn't far-fetched. Fred had strangled a man. He'd wanted to kill. It was possible Fred had come to my office prepared for a fight. At the moment, I wanted to cancel the Lock-in, defy my Brother, and close the church for good.

—No, I don't understand, I told him. Did you steal their drugs?

—God wants the Lock-in to happen. The children need this.

—The children need our attention, our unconditional love.

I'd go home that night to find Elizabeth covered in blood. I would hear from Rachel about how my daughter and Nelle had torn Fred's studio apart. Lourna and I would take Elizabeth to the hospital and we'd have her admitted to Warm Springs.

—There's a lot of evil in this world, my Brother. They just want to feel safe.

—Don't I know it.

I would expect a call from Lester that night. I had to get him the money. I had to wait for the bank to open so I could go see how much cash I could withdraw, whether I qualified for a loan, but I expected Lester and his men would find me before any of that happened. I had less than twenty-four hours to collect twelve thousand dollars. Impossible. Even if every member of our congregation agreed to donate a set amount, I'd never raise the funds in time.

—I'm not here to judge you, I said, but if you stole from the Alejandro Brothers, I need to know. God wants to help, but He helps us in His Time. According to His Plans.

—My plan is to perform sweet music for the Children of God.

SO NOW YOU SEE

Why I needed to tell ~~your mom~~ Rachel to get everyone out of Watershed? Why we needed to take him out? Fred had threatened Zach. Which I didn't know at the time, but based on what's happened, you have to understand. Fred had stabbed Lester. He tried to drown me. Now he had a gun. Don't think we forgot about the gun, Nelle. That's right. Zach says he kicked the Browning Hi-Power between the ivy plants? A loaded gun, on the floor, and nobody bothers to recover it? You don't think Fred actually left the office without it, do you?

Fred knew what he was doing. He said he didn't need to pray about it. A guy in a story like this doesn't walk off with a loaded pistol without the intention of using it to get what he wants. He didn't want to collect the cash for the Alejandro Brothers. He wanted bombs, he wanted *everyone* at the Lock-in, remember? Especially you and me, Nelle.

We had to kill Fred before he killed us.

Before Zach and Lourna came to pick me up Thursday, I told Rachel not to let anyone in the church Saturday night. —Something bad's gonna happen, I'm sure of it.

Rachel didn't reply. She was too focused on making sure you were okay. Running her hands over your face, counting every hair on your head, pressing her lips to your forehead. I know she heard me, though. Whether she believed me or not, Rachel got the children out. Like Zach said, No dead children in this story. Maybe Rachel forced a confession out of Fred, or maybe Fred talked in his sleep. Doesn't matter. What matters is he talked to me.

—Like I'm in any position to judge the mental stability of another human, I said to Rachel, but Fred was not well when he talked to me. He's going to blow up the church. He told me. You can't let anyone in there. I wiped the blood off my hands. I breathed. I sat on your porch and waited for my parents to collect me and take me to where I belonged.

Fred would need to master every detail of his plan. He'd need to pack the pews with enough explosives to blow the roof off the barn. One big blast, and then all-consuming fire. He'd need enough explosives to ensure nothing remained. No evidence. Not so much as a toothbrush. No teddy bears, not a comb. Nothing. I see him threading different-colored wires into balls of clay. I see him rigging a timer. Arming it. He's waiting, waiting while the timer ticks.

His possessive self won't allow him simply to leave. No, he's got to wait until everyone arrives. Let the children come unto me. He has to find a place to hide, though, because his presence will throw them off. He won't leave the church, not when he hears their laughter in the yard. He won't leave. He'll see his plan through to the end. And what better place to watch everyone drown in fire than in a trough full of water? What better place than underwater?

So he slips on his diver's mask, inserts the mouthpiece of his snorkel into his mouth, bites the rubber bit, holds the snorkel upright, and lowers himself into the trough. He cradles Lester's gun against his chest, as if it were some kind of flotation device, or a lead weight to hold him down. His coffin is cold and its cold hands lock around him. He slides under.

Now the ribbed dome of the water's surface shimmers above him. All he hears is the cavernous sound of his own breath. He doesn't hear the explosion until after the surface turns bright red, the giant eyelid crashing over him in wave after wave of fire. Pieces of the roof come smoldering down, hissing onto his eyelid. He can't breathe. He can't lift his head.

Samson brought down the temple of Dagon with his bare hands. Fred can't touch the walls of his temple to lift him. His hands recoil. Too hot. It's burning too fast. Where are the children? Where's Rachel? This is not how it was supposed to end. The water boils and the roof crashes through. Watershed burns around him. He's got to go, Nelle. You see him in the middle of it all? You see him writhing underwater? He set this thing in motion. It's his time.

THE PART WHERE LOURNA SAVES HER HUSBAND

The Bible says in Him we have redemption through His blood, through the forgiveness of our sins, according to the riches of His grace that He lavished upon us.

Lavish grace on your enemies, folks.

Saturday after the bombing, after I'd raced into the fire wrongly thinking I had to save the kids who'd participated in the Lock-in from burning to death, after the doctors treated me at a hospital in San Antonio for minor burns and smoke inhalation, after I visited patients in the burn ward while waiting for my wife, Sheriff Lufkin cornered me in my hospital room and asked many questions. Aside from the meeting with Lester in my office and a few other minor episodes, I told the sheriff everything I've told y'all today.

—Rachel knows more than she's letting on, Sheriff Lufkin said to me. I doubt if I'll get much more out of her, though. It's obvious she hates me.

—Sounds like that would bother you if she did. Hate you.

Sheriff Lufkin put on his cowboy hat but remained in his chair. For a moment it seemed he wanted to go over the details one more time, and I worried he'd press me on how Rachel managed to corral the kids into Freedom Keys before the bomb went off, how she seemed to know in advance something terrible would happen. Whatever had tipped off Rachel—Fred's odd behavior, his disappearance, his brutal attack on Lester—she didn't share it with the law.

—It *would* bother me, Sheriff Lufkin said. I got enough enemies. Finally he heaved himself out of his chair. —Medical staff will discharge you. At least you'll get to sleep in your own bed tonight. Lourna's outside. Y'all can go see your daughter.

— Thanks, I said. Between you and me, Rachel doesn't hate you.

The sheriff left, the door closed briefly before a nurse opened it, and Lourna came in wearing a white blouse, cashmere sweater, skirt, flats, and beautiful ankles. An aura of citrus. My heart skittered. Lord, I'd missed her. When Lourna reached my bed, she hugged me and kissed me on the lips and neck. The nurse told me to get into the wheelchair. I said are you kidding me, I've been walking around all day. She said protocol required my butt in the chair.

— Enjoy the free ride, Lourna said as the nurse unfolded the metal stirrups under my feet.

— Eighteen years with this man, Lourna told the nurse. You believe it? Here, honey. You're supposed to drink water. Lourna handed me a thirty-two ounce Big Gulp.

— You and me, I said, and took a sip of icy water. And Elizabeth.

— You ready to see her?

— Yes, I've seen enough of everybody in here.

While Lourna rolled me down the hall, the reflected ceiling lights swam along the floor between my feet. The strips of light sluiced over the linoleum, and a voice in me wanted to ask Fred if he could recreate the effect on our stage. In the coming weeks, while the investigation played out, during my sermons at the conference room at Fair Weather Inn, our temporary home while we awaited the next Watershed Project, and especially at rehearsals, I'd catch myself asking Fred a question or two about the sound or lighting system. I've made the mistake of calling our new keyboardist "Fred" more than once. Luckily, the new guy doesn't mind.

We rode the elevator to the ground floor. I was wondering if the sheriff and his deputies would escort us to the car, but I didn't see them in the elevator or in the lobby.

Warm Springs was located in the same medical center, but you had to leave St. Luke's through the lobby, exit the double-glass doors, and cross the street to get to the parking garage. They had a pedestrian lane and a skywalk, like at airports. I didn't notice Lourna's purse. The concrete rolled under my feet, and the white stripes marking the pedestrian lane blurred together.

For my burns, the doctor had given me painkillers. Rachel could've told you the brand.

We were about half way to the other side of the street when a van skidded into the crosswalk. The driver's door flew open. Lester Hargreve jumped out with one hand buried in a cast, the other holding a pistol pointed at my head. This would be the last time Lester Hargreve pulled a gun on a man of the Lord.

I didn't see Lourna reach into her purse.

—Sorry, Lester said. Alejandros are taking a big loss. It would've been me.

Before I could reply, I felt myself tip sideways, and I landed on my hip with the wheels facing Lester. I heard gunshots. I assumed Lester was shooting at me. On account of his shattered wrist, his aim was poor, but I figured he would eventually hit me, so I prepared for my eternal rest. I crawled forward on my knees and elbows, and when I looked up, Lourna stood with a pistol aimed at Lester Hargreve.

—Lourna?

She nodded without taking her eyes off her target. The gun in Lester's hand sank toward the street. His mouth moved and his eyelids closed. I thought I saw a spot of blood at the base of his throat, like the rose I'd seen on Rachel's throat in the music room, and I saw real blood spread from the hole in his neck down the length of his paisley shirt. The bartender with sea legs dropped to his knees, his jaw went slack, and he tilted his head against the door's edge.

He died in the street. My wife killed him.

The official report would state Sheriff Lufkin and his deputies hadn't seen Hargreve. They'd reached the curb by the time they heard shots fired, but the van and a concrete pillar beneath the skywalk blocked their view of the actual shootout.

I'm not sure what really happened. It could be the sheriff saw Lester pull his gun and froze. It could be the sheriff saw my wife shoot

Lester, and by the time the sheriff could think what to do the whole thing was over. I lay on my back in the middle of the crosswalk.

A few cars honked their horns.

Slowly Lourna returned her tiny pistol to her purse and lowered the purse to the street and slid it away from her and raised her hands in the air as the sheriff and his deputies jogged toward us with weapons drawn. They checked the van. No one else was inside. One of the deputies kicked Lester's gun out of his hand. Before it quit, Lester's body swayed like a reed.

I GET THE LAST WORD HERE

Zach and Lourna would spend the next several hours at the sheriff's office, answering questions, and by the time they were done, visiting hours at Warm Springs had ended.

Zach visited me the next day. I suspected he might read my letter, Nelle, so I prepared a trap for him. We sat at a table in the cafeteria by the window. Warm Springs offered self-serve coffee, regular and decaf, on a moveable cart, but Zach wasn't interested.

—Your psychiatrist thinks it'd be best if you stayed a few more days. Is that all right with you, Elizabeth? If you stayed a few more days?

—Sure, book me for the month. I don't care.

—Why don't you care, Elizabeth?

—My name's not Elizabeth anymore. It's Elena.

—Okay, Elena. Don't you want to get better?

—Why can't Jesus heal me? He's supposed to work miracles.

—What've you been reading? Anything good?

Normally I didn't take my *Webster's* to the cafeteria. I preferred to read in my room unless my roommate was in there with the TV on, then I'd go to the common room and sit by the window and let my eyes run over the page until I felt like sleeping. For Zach's visit, I'd taken a news clipping and tucked it inside the dictionary.

—It's not a good story, I told Zach. It doesn't have a happy ending.

—Not all good stories have happy endings. Can I take a look?

I took the newspaper out of the dictionary and slid the page towards him across the table. I'd folded the newspaper into fourths until only the text showed. Each paragraph I'd circled with a pencil. I'd have preferred a highlighter or a blue pen, but all they let us use in here are these stubby orange pencils without erasers, like the kind next to the card catalogs at the library.

Zach glanced at the headline and winced. He sat up like someone had turned a screw in his spine. He moved his lips as he read, and the worry passed over his face. Not worry for the people in the news article, but for my reaction to his worry. My trap forced him to stomach some bad news under the gaze of his daughter, a story that according to his daughter made a pretty good case for why God doesn't exist. Why no almighty creator sees you or anyone in your mother's womb. —And if he does, I'd like you to help me understand, Zach, how he can plan these things and still live with himself?

Nelle, can you believe Zach tried to prevent the news from being read on air? He argued with the radio producer, saying he could "skip the story," claiming it might be disturbing and inappropriate for some listeners. When the broadcast came out, he cut the part where he reads the story, but thankfully I'm here to put it back in. Told you, Nelle, I get the last word here.

THE NEWS STORY ZACH DIDN'T WANT TO READ ON THE AIR

Wyatt Hasselbach, the father of a child found dead in her own roach-infested crib, will spend the rest of his life in prison. Last month, a jury convicted Hasselbach of first-degree murder, a conviction that carries a mandatory sentence of life in prison without the possibility of parole.

Three-month-old Layla Hasselbach died of malnutrition and dehydration after being left tied to the bars of her crib with a jump rope for up to two weeks in November of 1991. She was only a few ounces more than her birth weight at the time of her death. Hasselbach blames his daughter's death on Layla's mother, Kamila Mazur, who will stand trial on charges of first-degree murder and child endangerment resulting in death beginning April 12th in Salterra, TX.

GOD GETS DOWNGRADED TO LOWERCASE LETTERS

—It's horrible, sweetheart. It happened in our town, as a consequence of illegal activity, beneath the surface of our town. Listen, I don't know if they've told you yet, but Watershed is gone. Our church burnt to the ground in a fire.

—These two "parents" could have been shooting up with the Alejandro Brothers. With drugs stored in our church. Instead of caring for Layla.

—I completely agree. Fires, earthquakes, tsunamis. Thousands die, and we forget because we respond to stories, not statistics. I hear you, sweetheart. This one got to you, I'm sorry. I have some other news, about your mom, she's safe. I understand how this makes you angry.

—I'm not angry. I leaned back in my chair. —I'm curious. Did your god have a plan for Layla? Did your god turn Layla's parents into drug addicts so they could tie her up in her crib and abandon her? Covered in roaches? Did your god plan for the cockroaches?

—I love you, sweetheart. I'm sorry. Your mom and I can't wait for you to come home.

—What if I don't want to come home?

—What d'you mean? Zach's face dropped. He knew what I meant. His body tensed. The threat of my indifference got to him, the way Layla's death got to me. Forget the church, whatever "other news" he had to share.

When Zach looked up, his shoulders had relaxed and he was crying.

—I'm sorry about everything. He got up and hobbled past the table and hugged me. I hugged him back and we both cried, and I could smell his aftershave and a faint hint of smoke and felt the rough spots where he'd messed up his morning ritual with that plastic razor, unable to locate his good one, my friend, and I would be lying Nelle if I didn't admit, while we sat at Warm Springs, before he could tell me about your dad, us crying and holding each other, I experienced the relief I'd been looking for the time I cut myself in the car, the kind that lasts and doesn't require pain as its starting point.

—Stay with us, he said.

—Okay, I said. I'll do that.

It seemed possible. I could obey his request, and I wouldn't put an expiration date on it. You and I have expiration dates. Fred had an expiration date. Layla had one. Zach has one. *Webster's* tells me "expiration" means "the last emission of breath," or "the act or process of releasing air from the lungs." Maybe after Zach expires and I'm so old I've forgotten who made the request and when and where, I will still be able to give back instead of in by honoring what he said to me in the cafeteria. *Stay with us.*

And then, as if to really drive home his point, Zach led me to the window, where down below in the parking lot, my mother stood by our car with Shadow in her arms. My Shadow, complete with pink tongue, floppy charcoal ears, and the bald patch on her hind leg where her buckshot wound had scarred over.

I waved. They couldn't see me behind the reflection in the glass. Shadow ran a circle around my mother and wrapped the leash around her legs. Shadow's tail resembled an abused pipe cleaner, but otherwise she seemed good. She looked happy. She'd survived.

—Are you going to read Layla's story on the radio? I asked Zach.

—I might not read it out loud if that's okay.

—That's okay, Zach. Did you catch the trial date? Monday after Easter. I smiled, and I rocked in my chair. —It's nice to have something to look forward to.

After what I did to Fred's studio, I was probably still crazy in Zach's eyes, and he couldn't tell me who'd died, what really happened to the church, and what Mom did, but I was his teenage daughter, still fluent in the language of rebellion.

—Absolutely not, he said.

—I want to go to the trial, Zach.

—Never.

—I want to be there. I think it'd be *good* for me.
—No, sweetheart.
—Please, *Dad*?
—When you come home, we'll talk about it with your mother.
—Okay. What else did you need to tell me?

A BADASS REDEMPTION STORY

Layla and Fred died, and yet on New Year's Eve in 1984, Rick Allen, drummer for Def Leppard, got into a car accident with his girlfriend and severed his left arm. He rebuilt his drum kit by adding extra pedals for his left foot, the same effects he would have played on the drums with his arm had he not lost it in the accident. So he plays drums with only one arm and still sounds awesome. The world is full of badass redemption stories.

Normally in this part of the sermon, you'd hear me say "in closing," which is my signal to the keyboardist to get his butt on stage and start playing light background music while I wrap up my sermon. I say "in closing," but I don't close anything. I'm leaning hard on the Holy Spirit to deliver salvation. You'd be surprised how some light background music—I say "light background," but what I'm talking about is a specific chord progression in a major key with an "amen" or "plagal" cadence, and if I want my keyboardist to keep playing, I will make a signal with my left hand, I'll twirl my index finger behind my back. I do this while I'm still talking. You'd be amazed how the light piano fires up my congregation.

I signal for the keyboardist to play, and I invite my Prayer Partners up to the alter, and I call upon anyone out there who needs a breakthrough, a miracle, a healing touch.

—Come on up, y'all.

If you're in need of that job offer, if you're praying for that cancer to go into remission, if you want that son to come home from the war, if you want that daughter to come home from the ward, anyone out there in need, y'all come up on here, and we're gonna pray for you.

And then Rachel enters the stage and starts singing "Up to the Altar." Fred knew how to switch to whatever key she wanted, he played with total freedom, and he'd throw her all the right chords, and he always made the transition from playing solo to backing her on vocals so smooth you wouldn't notice. And I don't care what our other female vocalists said about her not always singing in key. Rachel's got a lovely voice. She's not afraid of putting herself out there.

She's not afraid.

In closing, we're a small church down at the end of Franklin Road. To get there, you start out on Main, head south, drive past Annie's Antiques and the DQ. If you think you've gone too far, you're wrong. You're only getting started. You turn left onto the rutted road after the windmill. That's Franklin. You'll find us at the end. Tonight, since we're on the air, I'm gonna fall on my knees and fold my hands. We don't have a big stage in this studio, but you'll imagine one with me, won't you? You've come this far, might as well go all the way.

—Lord, hear our prayer.

And I do realize by confessing what all transpired at my church, confessing live, I am incriminating myself and will likely spend a long time in jail. Or not. Remember, the Alejandro Brothers are still out there, they could put a bullet in my head, or not. I could destroy the tapes of this broadcast, but someone out there might have taped my confession, or not. Maybe the cartel is listening, maybe not. Maybe Sheriff Lufkin's listening, or not. So you folks realize, I haven't "closed" anything. Wait, you'll see. We're not wrapping this burrito yet.

It's like in Psalm 27 when David asks of the Lord if he can live in the house of the Lord all the days of his life. That's what we're after, friends. That's the goal of heaven. Not the Clouds-and-Pearly-Gates stuff. It's about living beside the Lord. I promise, you're gonna be grateful you took the time to live in the Lord with us tomorrow. We've taken care of the toilet leak in the women's restroom. And the neighbors are putting out cans of Purina behind the music school to attract more cats, so I can *almost* guarantee we'll no longer have the mice problem.

AFTER THE NIGHT WATERSHED WENT UP IN FLAMES

I took some time off from preaching to stay with my daughter and help my wife recover from the trauma of shooting Lester Hargreve. Not much, though. I like to work. Three weeks later, I was back preaching out of the conference room at the Fair Weather Inn on I-10. Naturally, it was a smaller crowd. Most of our flock had stayed home to await the next Watershed, but we'd get everyone back. We would all be together again real soon.

One day, after shaking hands with the last of our worshipers, a man in a black coat and tie and sunglasses escorted me outside to the alley behind the inn. I was thinking of the final scene in the mafia movie where you get the last witness in the alley with a bullet in his forehead and the bird's-eye shot of him on his back. Trail of blood, twitching limbs.

The dark-suit guy said nothing, and I wasn't thinking of resisting, but before he could pull out his gun, for some reason I found myself talking to Fred Valenkemp's ghost: Sorry, Brother. You expected some alone-time with your wife in heaven before I got there. I understand. I regret to inform you that your wife is *alive*. She's alive and well and still working for me, Pastor Zacharias P. Hembrey. Everyone survived except you, Fred.

Which leads me to my next point: I doubt you ended up in heaven, but if you did, I further regret to inform you, *I'm probably about to get shot*, so it will be you and *me* waiting on Rachel for what I hope will be a very long time. I don't know why you did what you did, whether you think you're my enemy or not, but I forgive you, my Brother.

While I was rambling in my head, someone tapped me on the shoulder. I opened my eyes. Alejandro the Elder was short, bald, and wore small round glasses. The guy in the suit, his driver, had disappeared. The alley was silent, save for a few crickets talking in the weeds. Beer bottles, cigarette butts, a faint smell of kitchen grease. He wore blue jeans, cowboy boots, and a denim shirt with a turquoise bolo. Heavy gold rings on his fingers. A tiny black skull painted onto the long nail of his right pinky.

—We're glad Lester's gone, Alejandro the Elder said. He hooked his thumbs behind his belt, turned his boot-heel in the gravel as if to mimic the sound of a life extinguished. —We can rebuild churches. We can rebuild anything in this business. Except trust. Never steal from your father. Alejandro the Elder wagged his finger at me and walked back to the street.

Guess I'm not giving anything away by saying he didn't kill me. But after recovering from the shock of not being dead, I did have a question.

—Excuse me? *Una pregunta, por favor*?

He stopped, turned, and stared at me impatiently.

—Of all the churches in Texas, why did y'all choose mine?

Alejandro the Elder reached into his pocket and waved a one-hundred-dollar bill.

—The green ticket. He gets you anywhere. I like this man, your president.

I didn't understand, but I nodded anyway. I think he meant "Ben Franklin"? Since our church was at the end of "Franklin" Road? Surely there were other, better roads. Before I could speak, a car pulled up, and he got inside and the car drove him away. Of course, I would not have informed him Ben Franklin was never our president.

EPILOGUE: WHAT WE CAN SAY ABOUT EACH OTHER NOW

ZACHARIAS: "The Lord bless you and keep you. The Lord make his face shine upon you and be gracious unto you. The Lord look upon you with favor and give you peace. Amen." I can't guess what lessons, if any, my daughter learned. I wouldn't presume, or whatever. She's home now, and at least we're talking. I believe we appear to be on the same page.

ELIZABETH: If we're talking about what my dad learned, I'd say he learned he's not slick enough to serve two lords at once. As for me, I believe, like—jeez, honestly, I'm gonna have to think about it. Can I have some more time?

ACKNOWLEDGMENTS

I would like to express my deepest thanks to my friends and fellow writers who offered their excellent feedback on this book and who've provided advice, encouragement, and good cheer over the years: John Dufresne, Karen Kravit, Teddy Jones, Cully Perlman, Scott Jones, Jill Coupe, Peter Stravlo, William Jensen, Danielle LeBlanc, Rosanne Braslow, Harry Hawkins, Sue Garman, Melissa Bergum, Andrew Stimpson, Lizette Strait, and Alan Bahr. Huge thanks to my agent, Jonathan Agin, for helping me get this book into shape and into the world. Thank you to Reagan Rothe and everyone at Black Rose Writing for giving my novel a home. Thank you to Murph Davis, Tony Pena, Rachel Pena, Anthony Guzman, Andrew King, Al Stauder, Harvey Dickens, Dane Bonecutter, Dick Buhl, and everyone at River City. Special thanks to my family for their love and support: Eleanor, Kyle, John, Valerie, Ana, Doug, Ale, Chris, Landy; my parents, James and Alice; my sons, James and Caleb; my wife, Rocío; and our Blue Weimaraner, Georgia, who gets us out the door and keeps our lives interesting. Thank you all.

ABOUT THE AUTHOR

David Norman's debut novel, *South of Hannah*, received the Impress Prize Commendation Award and was published by Impress Books in 2018. His stories have appeared in *Gulf Stream*, *American Literary Review*, *Image*, *Southern Humanities Review*, *Rio Grande Review*, and many other publications. David Norman performs as lead pianist for the River City Band, a jazz orchestra in San Antonio, Texas, and he teaches writing at Trinity University. Learn more about his writing and music at www.davidrnorman.com.

NOTE FROM THE AUTHOR

Word-of-mouth is crucial for any author to succeed. If you enjoyed *The Watershed Project*, please leave a review online—anywhere you are able. Even if it's just a sentence or two. It would make all the difference and would be very much appreciated.

Thanks!
David Norman

Thank you so much for checking out one of our **Literary Fiction** novels.
If you enjoy this book, please check out our recommended title for your next great read!

The Five Wishes of Mr. Murray McBride by Joe Siple

2018 Maxy Award "Book of the Year"

"A sweet...tale of human connection...will feel familiar to fans of Hallmark movies." *–KIRKUS REVIEWS*

"An emotional story that will leave readers meditating on the life-saving magic of kindness." *–IndieReader*